RECKONINGS

Sydney Campbell

ISBN: 978-1-7774505-4-0

Cover design by abu-chan
Editing by Megan Records

For Mr. Campbell. He puts up with a lot.

Other books by Sydney Campbell:

Allie Styles Romance Series:
Temptation (Book 1)
Deception (Book 2)
Reckonings (Book 3)
Beginnings (Book 4)

Courtyard Tales of Contemporary Romance
Reawakening
Redemption
Reckless

CHAPTER ONE

It was an early February morning in Montreal, the sky clear, cloudless, and endlessly blue. It was easy to imagine just how freakishly cold it was outside. Looking out the window from my cozy bed, I shivered and pulled the duvet up to my chin.

For once, I had woken up before the alarm, and I was enjoying the scenery, both outside my window and beside me in bed. Fast asleep, Matt made for endless visual entertainment. Every time he took a breath, I'd watch his chest rise and fall, the exhale defining every muscular feature. He opened his eyes and smiled.

"What's up?" he mumbled, rolling over and wrapping his arm around me.

"Looks cold out there," I said.

"So don't get up," he said. "Lucky you, you have that luxury."

It was true. I did have that luxury. Working as a freelance writer afforded me all sorts of perks, especially now that I'd found a niche in erotica writing—a niche that paid very well. And allowed for some exquisite research, not to mention some questionable tax write-offs.

Matt and I had recently returned from four months in Amsterdam. I'd flown out to meet him on a whim while he was there on a consulting contract. The crazy part was we'd only known each other a few weeks before he left, and my getting on that plane had been a huge gamble. Luckily, it paid off.

We'd been home a few days, reluctant to leave the confines of the apartment. We were enjoying this artificial extension of our adventures abroad and I, for one, was not looking forward to returning to business as usual. I hadn't even told Lynn, my best friend, that I was home yet.

Matt worked as a network architect, often spending six months at a time in foreign locations on consulting gigs. He was due back at work on Monday, but it was only Friday, so I wasn't sure what he was going on about.

"And where do you have to be, exactly?" I

asked.

"I need to get my house in order. Literally. I'm back in the office on Monday and all my shit is still back at the apartment. I'm going to have to go over there today and clear it out."

I rolled over onto my side and propped myself up on my elbow, studying him for a moment.

"Have you spoken to Dave yet?" I asked.

"No."

"So, just, 'Surprise!'?" I asked.

"Something like that."

I nodded.

"Are you going to keep paying rent?"

"Of course I am. I'm not going to renege on that. And don't worry. I'll pay you rent, too."

"I'm not worried," I said. "I'll come with you."

Matt looked at me.

"You sure?" he asked.

I nodded.

"I'm not ready to let you out of my sight just yet. Let's walk Loki and we'll go."

*

We pulled up outside Matt's building, which sat on a pretty, tree-lined street in an upscale neighbourhood. He'd just moved into the place a few months before leaving for Amsterdam. Knowing he'd be spending a lot of time abroad, he moved in with two friends, Dave and Pete, and took a tiny bedroom to keep as a pied-a-terre for when he was in town. It was all ideal, except for the fact that I met Matt through Pete...while Pete and I were dating. The situation made for a very sticky start, but now that Pete was in a serious relationship with a woman named Diana, all was right with the world.

We got out of the car and as we walked up to the front door, Matt turned to me.

"Nervous?" he asked.

"A little," I admitted, laughing. "I don't know why. There was really nothing between Pete and me. It still feels a little weird."

Matt took my hand and squeezed it.

"I get it," he said. "But don't worry. He's probably not even home."

"Good point," I said. "Wanna fuck in his room?"

Matt turned to me.

"Allie!"

"Kidding. But maybe we can fuck in your room?" I asked, flashing a mischievous grin.

"Now that it is a definite possibility."

He pulled me close and kissed me deeply, making my head swim. And then, as he worked his key in the lock, the butterflies settled down. But he'd stirred something in me and I was anxious to get inside.

By the time we were in his apartment, I was practically clutching at him. He laughed and put his finger to his lips as he looked around to see if anyone was home. There wasn't a sound in the apartment, and as we moved through the hallway, we could see both bedroom doors open. He turned around and shrugged.

"I guess the coast is clear," he said.

We continued through to the kitchen, and I stopped at the fridge to get a bottle of water.

"Go on," I said. "And you better be naked by the time I get in there."

Matt laughed and opened the door to his bedroom, which he then quickly shut. He turned to me, trying to arrange his face into a casual expression, something he was clearly having trouble with.

"What is it?" I said. "I don't care if it's a mess. You've seen my place. Hell, we lived together for four months."

"Um, Allie..." he started.

But before he could say anything else, the door to Matt's room opened again, and Dave emerged, wearing only his boxers. His eyes lit up at the sight of me.

"Allie!" he said, a little louder than was

necessary.

"Hey, Dave. Whatcha doing?" I asked.

Dave looked at me, then Matt. He clapped Matt on the shoulder.

"Great to see, buddy. We missed you."

Matt smiled and clapped Dave's shoulder in return.

"It's good to be home," Matt said.

And then the door opened a little further, and much to my surprise, Lynn walked out, wearing Dave's robe. My jaw dropped before the message hit my brain, so part of me was so excited to see her, while the other part was in complete shock.

"Lynn!" I said.

Lynn walked over to me, looking sheepish. She raised her eyebrows and tilted her head to the side, silently begging forgiveness. In truth, there was nothing to forgive. During one of our FaceTime chats while I was in Amsterdam, Lynn had confided that she was seeing someone, but not yet ready to tell me who it was. I didn't push it, because I'd done the exact same thing to her with Matt. So how could I be upset with her now? Why they were messing around in Matt's room, I had no idea, but whatever.

I threw my arms around her and held her tight. For over fifteen years, this woman had been my rock, my cheerleader, and my very best friend. We rarely fought, and we had never spent four months apart. It was like I found a piece of me again that I hadn't realized was missing. As she returned the hug, it was like I was made whole again.

"I missed you so much," I whispered in her ear.

"Me, too. I'm so glad you're home," she said.

I turned my head slightly to see what the boys were up to, and saw them chatting and catching up, clearly relieved there would be no girl drama. I turned back to Lynn and whispered.

"Is he any good?"

She burst out laughing and nodded enthusiastically.

"Although, based on your recent columns, I may be coming to you for some tips on some things," she said.

I just laughed.

The four of us migrated over to the kitchen table and Matt, Lynn, and I sat down while Dave rustled up some drinks and snacks. We spent some time telling them about Amsterdam, me going on about art and food while Matt talked tech and the challenges of his contract.

"So? How did you two hook up?" I asked

when there was a lull in the conversation.

Lynn and Dave looked at each other. I'd known Dave a long time. He worked in the music industry, and our paths would often cross as I was working as a food critic. We'd see each other at openings and events. He and Matt had known each other since childhood, had studied together, and it was always assumed that Dave would also pursue a career in tech, but the glamour of show biz was too much for him to resist. From what I could recall, he must have been around 33 years old. Lynn was my age, 31, with Matt leading us all by a nose at 34.

At that moment, it looked as if they were deciding what they wanted to tell us, already an invisible secret language clearly developed between the two of them. *This must be serious.* Lynn hadn't been in a relationship in years. She was not a tie-me-down kind of girl. Well, in the commitment sense. I had no idea about the other sense. Well, I had my ideas, but… anyway. Eventually, Lynn just threw up her hands at Dave and looked at me, point-blank.

"You wrote about his scar," Lynn said.

"What?" I said, confused.

Dave put his hand on Lynn's. She was clearly flustered and looking very guilty.

"Your column, Allie," Dave said. "She's

talking about your column."

I tried to remain calm.

"What are you talking about, Dave?" I asked.

Dave just rolled his eyes.

"Allie. I know you're Temple Fraser. And Lynn didn't tell me."

I shot a look at Matt.

"And Matt didn't tell me, either," Dave continued. "In one of the pieces, you wrote about the scar over his eye. I've known Matt since we were kids. I know that scar."

I sighed and closed my eyes.

"We bumped into each other downtown one night," Lynn said, picking up the thread of the story. "I'd had a few drinks, and so had Dave. Neither of us was drunk, but we were definitely a little loose-lipped, and I'm sorry. But he asked me, straight out, if you were Temple Fraser. I tried to deny it, but he just knew. He swore he wouldn't say a word, and he hasn't, right Dave?"

Dave shook his head, he hadn't.

"Anyway," Lynn continued. "We ended up chatting all night. We knew each other through you, Allie, but we'd never really gotten to know each other before. I'm actually a little pissed you never fixed us up before."

I raised my eyebrows and looked pointedly

at Dave.

"To be honest, I didn't think you'd be his type."

Dave looked sheepish.

"It's true," Dave said. "I have had some awful taste in women, and some horrible judgment. I will forever be thankful for one night at a bar with this woman."

With that, he leaned over and kissed Lynn. It was nice to see.

*

Matt and I walked out the front door of the building, each of us holding a few of his bags. I had been surprised he didn't want to bring his own pillow, but he sheepishly admitted my bedding was far superior to his, and he was happy to leave it behind. Little things like this amused me. Not that he felt them, but that he admitted them. It was incredibly charming.

"So what do you think about that?" Matt asked, breaking my reverie.

I turned to him as we walked through the snow-covered sidewalk, towards the car.

"I'm happy for them. If Dave is truly changed, I think they're a great match. He's a great guy. Just, like he said, he's had horrible taste in women. Always the flashy ones, which is fine, but he liked the ones with no substance. Dave needs a woman. A strong woman. Like Lynn. It'll be great."

Matt nods.

"Well, you obviously know her better than I do. But from the little I've seen, I'd have to agree. Okay. Let's get this stuff back to your apartment."

"Our apartment."

Matt smiled at me, then leaned down to kiss the top of my head.

"Our apartment. Weird. Okay. So, what do you want to do today?"

"Well," I started. "To tell you the truth, I'm still kind of horny."

Matt laughed.

"When are you not?"

I rolled my eyes.

"I know, I know. But it's been pretty intense. And then Dave in his boxers—he's pretty ripped, you know."

Matt eyed me suspiciously.

"Don't you be getting any ideas," he said. "I am not into a foursome with Dave and Lynn."

I looked at him, horrified.

"Oh, no. Please erase that image from my mind. Fuck, Matt. That is something I can't unsee."

"Listen, Allie. It's something I DID see.

Remember? I opened the door."

"Oh, dear Lord," I said, remembering. "That's almost like walking in on your parents."

"Tell me about it."

"Hey! Matt! Our best friends are dating."

He laughed. I unlocked the car and we both climbed in. I put the keys in the ignition as we buckled up. I checked the side view mirror and was pulling out of the parking spot when Matt turned to me.

"Can I take pictures of you?"

I slammed on the brakes, narrowly missing the parked car in front of me. The car stalled and I restarted the engine. Matt broke out into nervous laughter.

"Sorry," he said. "Bad timing."

I cocked my head and put the car back into gear.

"I'm assuming you mean naked pictures."

"I do."

"While the idea of that is incredibly hot, I'm a little nervous about the execution," I admitted.

"Fair enough. Let's discuss it when you aren't driving."

I smiled at the road ahead of me, then felt his hand land on my knee. It slowly moved up my leg and I shifted gears.

"Matthew Goldberg. I am driving on icy Quebec roads. You would do well to remove that hand."

He did as instructed and gave me a quick salute.

"You can drive next time," I muttered.

"What are you so pissy about?" he asked.

"I am not pissy," I replied calmly. "I am hot and bothered. You knew that when we got in the car. Then you start talking dirty to me, putting a hand on my leg, and you expect me to concentrate on the road. It's incredibly cruel. Next time, you drive."

"Pull over."

I looked at him.

"Pull over," he repeated.

I pulled the car over and we both unclipped our seat belts. I reached to open my door, and he stopped me.

"No. Don't go anywhere. Just turn the keys one notch. Keep the seat heater on. Lower your pants."

I looked at him, incredulous.

"It's minus twelve outside."

"We're inside."

"It's broad daylight."

"There's no one around."

I looked around. It was true. My belly did a little flip flop and I reached down to undo my jeans. I slid my hands under the waist and pushed them down, raising my hips to do so and the lowering myself back down again on the warm seat, pants around my knees. I looked up at Matt. He gave me a lascivious grin. He moved toward me, raising the centre console, and kissed me. I wrapped my arms around his neck, savouring the feel of his lips on mine as a million fireworks went off in my head.

From the first time he kissed me, eight months earlier, I knew Matt was special. No one had ever kissed me like that before, as if he understood what lay deep inside me, and knew exactly how to reach it. The sex had been incredible from the start. After some exploratory, hands-on research and a few well-timed questions, he was the first man to ever make me come during intercourse, something I did regularly now.

And I knew I had the same effect on him. All I had to do was touch him, or even look at him in a certain way, and he'd be hard in an instant. I could make him last, or I could make him come within strokes. We were perfectly synced in bed. This made exploring new avenues extremely fun. There was complete trust. In fact, after a pretty big fight in Amsterdam, Matt presented me with a strap-on, turning a throwaway joke between us into a sincere apology. We haven't used it yet, but I loved knowing the option was there. In fact, I'd been thinking of procuring some Molly for my birthday. I'd never tried it before, but I was pretty sure Matt had, and I knew it would be the perfect way to lift those final inhibitions.

Matt pulled back, looking at me, somewhat puzzled.

"Something wrong?" he asked.

"Not at all," I murmured. "Just having some pleasant thoughts."

"Come back to me," he whispered and kissed me again.

I lost myself in that kiss, and as if from a faraway place, I felt his hands move downward, exploring my body, my breasts. He unzipped my jacket and slid his hands inside, down the front of my shirt, and cupped one breast in his palm. The warmth of his hand and the pressure against my nipple was enough to make me moan, and he put his other hand on my cheek and pulled away slightly. He looked deep into my eyes, his want plain to see, and lifted his finger to my mouth. I obliged him with a quick lick.

"Completely unnecessary," I said, spreading my legs so he could verify for himself.

His hand found its way, and his lips brushed

my ear as he whispered to me.

"God, Allie, so many months and you still get so wet, so fast."

"It's all you, Matt."

He slid a finger inside me, reaching deep and then pulling it out again. The next time, it was two fingers, and he used his thumb to make slow circles on my clitoris.

"I get so turned on making you come," he whispered.

"Keep talking," I moaned.

"You are just so hot. The noises you make, the way your body moves, the way your ass rises to meet me when I fuck you from behind."

"Matt..."

He increased the pressure on his thumb, and I felt the orgasm build deep inside my body. My mind blocked out everything but the pure ecstasy that was spreading through me. In that moment, I would've done anything for him. I was completely under his power.

"Come for me, Allie. I can feel how close you are."

I came violently, shuddering around his hand and grasping onto his neck. I bit his ear, causing him to let out a quick yelp which he followed up with an embarrassed laugh. When my body returned to something resembling normal, I raised my hips and pulled up my jeans. I looked over at him. He grinned.

"Start the car," he said.

"What about you? Don't you want me to take care of you?"

"Start the car," he repeated. "I'm going to jerk off while I watch you switch gears. It's hot as hell."

CHAPTER TWO

I woke slowly from the most delicious dream in which I was being bathed, warm water cascading down my chest. I looked around, puzzled by the fact that it was still dark and that I still felt warmth on my chest. I looked down to see Matt's hands, moving slowly over my breasts. I turned around, trying to prepare a witty comment about Mr. Consent feeling me up in my sleep when I realized he was also fast asleep.

I almost laughed out loud. I wondered what the ethics were in this situation. He wasn't the one being assaulted, I was, and I was wide awake. And willing. I slowly rolled over onto my back, ensuring he didn't lose his rhythm in the process. He was certainly having a good dream. Or, perhaps, milking cows. I closed my eyes and let my hand drift down between my legs. I must have sighed, or made one of my other apparently adorable noises because before I knew it, his mouth was on mine. I wrapped my hands around his waist, pulling him on top of me as I continued to kiss him.

"What's going on here?" he asked, amused.

"You tell me. I woke up to a pair of hands on my tits," I said.

"I was having the most incredible dream."

"Me, too."

We both laughed and then he kissed me again, working his hands through my hair, which was knotty after just a few hours' sleep.

"What time is it?" he asked.

"Fucking time," I replied.

I reached down and took hold of him, giving him a few good strokes, although he certainly didn't need it. I brought my knees up, spreading my legs and giving him room to settle between them. He braced himself against the mattress with his palms as I guided him in, and we both let out a little cry as he started to move. He tilted his hips, bringing his full length inside of me. It was one of the most exquisite feelings in the world, and I put my hands on his ass to hold him there for a moment.

"This feels so good," I murmured.

He leaned down and nuzzled my neck in response, kissing and nipping his way towards my mouth. We made out for a few seconds, until he could bear it no longer and started moving his hips again. I raised my ass to meet his every thrust. I took one hand off his ass, and reaching down, pressed my clitoris up against his cock as it moved in and out of me. I closed my eyes and arched my back, focusing all my energy on that one small spot where our bodies connected.

"Matt..."

"I got you, Allie."

He continued to move inside me, quickening his pace slightly, until I was almost panting. I was so close to the edge. I closed my eyes again and imagined him taking pictures of me like this, standing over me with a camera and me, with my legs spread, close to orgasm.

"Matt!" I screamed as I came once, then twice in quick succession.

I felt him speed up even more, and I tightened my muscles around him, wrapping my legs around his waist and pulling his head down to kiss me. He happily obliged as I took his lower lip between my teeth and bit down gently. I felt one final thrust and then he stilled as he came quietly but fiercely.

He collapsed on top of me, and after a moment he pulled out, rolling onto his back beside me.

"I hope this never gets old," I said.

He turned his head to look at me.

"How could it?" he asked.

My body was still pulsing. I lay there quietly for a few moments until everything calmed the fuck down. At 31, I'd had more than my fair share of sexual encounters, but I had never experienced anything like Matt. I often wondered if it was the same for him, but I was terrified to ask. If the answer was no, I didn't want to hear it. I'd already heard plenty about the ex-girlfriend who deflowered him. Chances are she was a much better lay than I was.

"What time is it?" Matt asked.

I turned my head and looked at my phone on the night table.

"Two o'clock," I said.

"Shit. I have to be in the office tomorrow. And now I'm starving."

"Want me to make you something?" I asked.

He kissed my forehead.

"I would love for you to make me something."

We got out of bed and went to the kitchen, not even bothering with clothes.

*

We stumbled into the kitchen and Matt sat down at the table while I opened the cabinet over the sink. I pulled out the weed box and handed it to him.

"Here," I said. "Make yourself useful. I don't think I've partied since we've been back from Amsterdam."

"True enough," he agreed. "And it will help me sleep after the snack. Clever girl."

He took the box from me and put it on the table, pushing aside the stacks of mail from the previous day. A bunch of them went over the edge, scattering across the floor. By this time, I was busy cracking eggs and decided to let him handle the cleanup.

"I assume omelets are okay," I said, my back to him as I poured the eggs into the frying pan.

He didn't say anything, so I turned to look at him. He was standing there, holding Josh's envelope in his hand. I turned off the heat on the stove.

"What's this?" he asked.

"That is a letter from Josh. It arrived while we were away."

"What does it say?" he asked.

"I don't know. If you look at the envelope,

you'll see it hasn't been opened."

"Why haven't you opened it?"

I sighed. I abandoned the eggs, took his hand, and led him back to the table. We both sat down.

"He called me while we were in Amsterdam. I didn't answer. So he sent a text message, which just said, *call me*. I deleted it. I never gave it another thought. Then, when we got home and when I was going through the mail, I saw the letter. I didn't want to throw it out in front of you, so I stuffed it away. I'm not interested in Josh. I'm interested in you."

Matt frowned, turning the envelope over in his hand.

"So, you're not the least bit curious to see what this says?" he asked.

"Not in the least," I assured him.

He sighed and put the envelope carefully on the table.

"Why didn't you answer his call? Or return his text?"

"I told you. I have no interest in him. I don't care what he has to say to me. We bumped into each other a while ago, maybe it stirred something up for him. For a hot second, I thought maybe he was calling to tell me he was dating Lynn."

Matt looked utterly confused at that.

"Never mind," I said. "Long story. In any case, it doesn't matter."

"But it does matter," Matt said quietly. "You never fell out of love with him. The relationship didn't have a natural end."

"Matt, for Christ's sake. Why are you stirring up trouble? There is nothing to talk about here."

He stood up and looked at me for a moment. Then looked at the letter.

"I'm not so sure," he said. "I'm going to bed."

And with that, he turned and left the room.

*

I sat at the table after Matt left and stared at the envelope. I really had no desire to open it. As far as I was concerned, that part of my life was over with. I had moved on. Sure, things had maybe cut a bit close when Josh and I bumped into each other over the summer, but that was then. This was now.

I let the letter sit a while longer while I pulled the box towards me and finished rolling the joint Matt had started. I found some matches and lit up, inhaling deeply and instantly missing the most excellent weed we'd enjoyed in Amsterdam. This was just not the same. Nevertheless, it did the trick as I sat there, trying to untangle the strands of my life that seemed to be colliding in this particular instant.

I smoked the joint down to the roach before I made a move towards the letter, picking it up and turning it over in my hands. Finally, I put the roach down in the ashtray and opened the envelope. I pulled out a single sheet, folded, unlined. On it was written: *Allie, I tried to call and text but got no answer. I just want to talk. Please call me. Josh.*

I got up and rummaged around in the junk drawer until I found a Sharpie. I sat back down at the table, and at the bottom of the letter I wrote, *Matt - I'm not interested. Please just drop it. Let's never mention it again.*

I left the letter unfolded on the table, so he'd be sure to see it in the morning. I emptied the ashtray, put it in the sink, and went to bed.

CHAPTER THREE

I woke the next morning to an empty bed. I wasn't particularly surprised. Matt hated arguments, and if he was still on edge about the previous night, it was totally his style to take off for work without waking me. I rolled towards his side and pulled his pillow close, giving it a good sniff, and then laughed at myself for the pure ridiculousness of that action.

I got up and wandered into the kitchen to put on the kettle for some tea. I glanced at the table and noted that the letter was gone. I picked up my phone and called Lynn.

"Hey," I said when she picked up. "Want to have lunch?"

"I so want to have lunch."

We made plans to meet, and I pulled on some sweats to take the dog for a walk.

*

I arrived at the restaurant and was shown to a table by the window. It was a cute little Mexican place in the Monkland area. Since it was located in the basement, the window was a real plus. But the food was excellent, and it was a spot I returned to again and again. I was needlessly perusing the menu when Lynn walked down the steps and approached the table. I jumped up and hugged her—it was the first time we had been alone together since I got home.

She took off her coat and we both sat down, opening our mouths to speak at once and then dissolving into laughter.

"Tell you what," I said. "Look at the menu first and then we'll chat."

"Good plan."

She picked up her menu, but when the waiter arrived, she closed it immediately and handed it to him politely. She then turned to me expectantly. I looked back at her, puzzled for a moment, then laughed.

"Maybe I neglected to mention it, but this is

not a working lunch. In fact, you're treating," I said.

"Ah," she said.

She gingerly plucked her menu back out of the waiter's hands and opened it up.

"Cactus salad, chorizo tacos, horchata."

The waiter nodded and looked at me.

"Times two," I said.

The waiter gone, Lynn turned to me, all business.

"So. Tell me. Are all those stories true? Because, holy shit, Allie, that's some crazy hot sex you've been having."

I shook my head and sighed.

"Lynn," I said. "If our friendship was a movie, it would fail the Bechdel test, you realize that, right?"

"Fuck that. Tell me about the Christmas market."

"No, you tell me about Dave. How's that going?"

Lynn smiled.

"Can you believe it?" she asked. "Me and Dave? I don't think I ever really looked twice at him before. And now? I can't look away."

Lynn blushed. A first.

"Holy cow," I said. "Blushing, huh? This is really something. The sex is good?"

"Oh, Allie. It's positively delightful. He's,

um, very creative."

"I love it. Maybe you'll give me some fodder."

"Maybe not!" she laughed, indignant.

The food came and we ate quietly for a while, though I broke the silence from time to time to tell her about some tasty Dutch food or an interesting sight I saw. By the time we hit dessert, we had moved fully off the topic of men and were catching up on life in general.

"Hey," Lynn said suddenly. "It's your birthday on Saturday! Got any plans?"

"Actually, I was going to talk to you about that."

"Go on," Lynn prodded.

"Any chance you could hook me up with Molly?"

Lynn looked at me appraisingly.

"Well, that's interesting," she said.

I just shrugged.

"Allie, you've never even expressed an interest in anything besides weed. Is Matt pressuring you into this?"

"What?" I asked. "Matt doesn't even know. It's a surprise. There's just some stuff I want to…try. You've done it, haven't you?"

"I have, and it's awesome. Highly recommend. The next day will suck, though. Prepare for that."

I nodded.

"Has he done it?" Lynn asked.

"I don't know. I assume he has. He's that kind of guy. I mean, not the kind who goes around taking e, but the kind of guy who's into trying shit at least once."

"I like him already," Lynn said.

It was only after I'd left the restaurant and was on the way home that I realized I hadn't even mentioned the letter from Josh. More proof that it really didn't matter to me.

*

I was standing outside Trish's apartment, leash in hand with Loki whining anxiously. She knew exactly who was inside. Trish opened the door and broke into a huge grin when she saw the dog.

"Puppy!" she squealed.

Loki jumped up on her (forbidden!) and licked her face while Trish laughed.

"Happy reunion," I said, smiling. "How'd you like to have a sleepover?"

"Oh, I'd love that!" Trish said. "Everything okay?"

"Fine. I just want a night alone with Matt. I might hit you up again on Saturday, if that's okay?"

"Of course it's okay! It's your birthday! And we're always happy to have Loki. My dad adores her."

I left her the leash and a bag of food and made my way back to my apartment. When I got inside, I looked around and noticed how much neater everything was now that Matt was living there. It had only been a few days but now everything seemed to have a place. I smiled to myself. This could work out very well for me. And then I remembered how we'd left things the night before, and wondered how I could fix them.

It wasn't like he was mad at me. And it didn't feel like jealousy on his part. Matt was not a jealous guy. For those reasons, I didn't think there was an actual problem between us that needed discussing or working through. At least not at the moment. With that in mind, I rolled a joint and then searched through one of my dresser drawers until I found what I was looking for. Then I took off all my clothes and sat down on the living room couch to wait for him to come home.

I lit up and slowly exhaled, watching the smoke curl around my head as it made its way into the air around me. I picked up the toy I had brought with me, a decent-sized purple vibrator—a trusty old friend. Not fancy, but a real workhorse. I rolled it between my fingers then turned it on, touching the tip lightly to my breast. I watched, with growing arousal, as my nipples hardened under the stimulation. I shifted a little on the couch, bringing the joint to my lips and inhaling deeply.

I took the vibrator and studied it for a moment. As the front door opened, I was just starting to trace a line on my leg, upwards from my knee. Matt walked in, shrugging off his coat, and stopped in his tracks when he saw me. He slowly put his coat on the closest chair and walked towards me. He dropped to his knees, and without saying a word, settled in at my feet. He took my little purple friend from my hand.

I put the joint in his mouth and he inhaled, smiling up at me as he did so. As he exhaled, he lightly touched the vibrator to my clitoris. I shuddered in response. He grinned at me again, then turned off the vibrator and put it aside.

"Whatcha doing?" he asked.

"Waiting for you," I replied.

He took the joint from my fingers and smoked for a bit, studying every inch of my body. I didn't move a muscle. Then he took his index finger and traced a line from my ankle up to my hip, wrapping his hand around the side of my waist.

"I like coming home and finding you naked," he said.

I shifted and spread my legs a little wider for him.

"I'm all yours."

Matt put the joint in the ashtray and slowly unbuttoned his shirt. He pulled it off and I reached forward to caress his shoulders. I closed my eyes at the feeling of his muscles beneath my palms. Both his hands were on my waist now, and I opened my eyes to find him leaning in to take my breast in his mouth. I moaned, giving him all the encouragement he needed to repeat the treatment on the other side.

He pulled away and looked at me, a slow smile spreading across his face. He picked up the vibrator and turned it back on.

"So," he said. "You were doing something like this?"

He ran the tip of the vibrator up the inside of my thigh, then made slow, lazy circles when he arrived at his destination.

"I hadn't gotten there yet..." I managed to get out.

"Hmm..." he said.

He brought the head between my legs and

slipped the vibrator inside, causing me to slide my ass down further on the couch, angling myself for maximum penetration.

"Classic Allie. No lube required."

I giggled until he shifted the vibrator, which caused me to once again grow very serious about the matter at hand. Or, rather, my matter in his hands. He slowly pulled it out, then used it to tease my sweet spot. I was writhing beneath him. It had been so long since I'd used anything electric and the intensity was overwhelming. And the fact that I wasn't controlling the vibrator added a whole other level of sexy to the scenario.

"You like this?" he asked.

"I do. A little to the left and I'll come in no time."

Matt obliged, and I followed through on my promise, a series of fireworks going off in my head as I did. When I settled, Matt put the vibrator aside and leaned in to kiss me—the first kiss we'd shared since our tiff the night before. It was deep and urgent, a clear longing in him to know that things were okay. I snaked my arms around his neck, sliding down off the couch to land in his lap.

"Men's clothing is very convenient," I said.

"You find?" he asked, humouring me.

"I do," I murmured, as I unzipped his

zipper and undid his button. "Look how convenient this is."

I proceeded to reach into his fly and find my way through his boxer briefs.

"Ah…there you are."

In no time at all, I not only had him free but fully at attention. I lifted one leg as I readjusted my position and then slid back down on top of him. He closed his eyes and sighed.

"You went how long without a girlfriend?" I asked, smirking.

"Too long. Too fucking long."

"Not a bad way to end the workday, is it?" I teased, moving slowly up and down.

"Shut up and ride me, woman."

The words sent a thrill down my spine and I picked up my speed, anchoring myself by holding tight to his shoulders. I'd learned over the past few months how to come like this, but I'd just gotten mine and I was far more focused on rocking his world. I changed my rhythm slightly and my mind drifted back to our last sexual encounter, the decision I'd made in my head, and how just the thought of it made me come so hard.

I once again picked up speed as I leaned down to whisper in his ear.

"You make me feel so fucking sexy, Matt. Every single part of me is on fire. I want you to take pictures of me. Naked."

"Oh, Jesus Christ."

Matt exploded into his orgasm, far surpassing any expectations I'd had. He grabbed my waist as he drove into me one last time, refusing to release me until his breathing had returned to normal. He swallowed, loosening his grasp, and smiled up at me. I kissed him.

"I think I love you," he said.

I answered him with another kiss.

CHAPTER FOUR

"So a little birdie told me you have a birthday coming up," Matt said.

We were sitting at the kitchen table the next morning, eating breakfast before he took off for work. I rolled my eyes. I had planned to surprise him on my birthday, but apparently someone had other plans.

"Let me guess, that bird's name is Lynn?"

Matt laughed.

"That obvious, huh? Why didn't you tell me?"

"Well, I didn't want you to make a fuss. There's only one thing I want for my birthday, and I'm in the process of arranging it."

Matt looked at me, puzzled.

"Do I get to know about it? Am I not involved in your birthday plans?"

"Of course you're involved in my birthday plans. This whole thing was supposed to be a surprise, but Lynn fucked up with good intentions."

"So I'm supposed to just trust you?" he asked.

Matt got up and brought his dishes to the sink, something I had never been in the habit of doing before he moved in. He dusted the toast crumbs off his shirt and looked at me.

"Yes, please. And kiss me before you go."

He smiled and walked towards me, leaning down to plant a nice juicy kiss on my mouth. I grabbed his collar.

"No," he said, firmly.

"Rawr," I replied.

He laughed and walked out of the kitchen. I sat there drinking my chai latte, listening for the click of the door. When I was sure he was gone, I picked up my phone and dialed.

"Lynn. I did not want him knowing it was my birthday," I said as soon as she picked up.

"But why? Don't you want a big romantic gesture?" she asked.

"No. I want to do Molly and fuck him up the ass."

There was sputtering and coughing on the

other end. I must have caught her sipping her morning coffee. When she was back under control, she took a deep breath.

"So I should cancel whatever plans I was making?" she asked.

"Yes, please."

"Noted."

"And get me the fucking Molly."

*

Hours later, I was still sitting at the kitchen table, but now with my laptop in front of me. I had my headphones in, with The Weeknd singing about being a motherfucking starboy. I was deep into the juicy bits of my latest story.

He came up behind me in the bathroom as I was standing over the sink, brushing my teeth. I felt his hands slide around my waist and he lifted my shirt over my head. We stood there, looking at our reflections in the mirror, our breaths short as our arousal grew. He lifted one hand and cupped my breast-

I was startled out of my work trance by Matt's hand, which had found its way to my breast as he read over my shoulder. I pulled out my earbuds and turned to look at him. He had just come in from work, and I had been completely oblivious—no doubt a combination of my activity and the blaring music.

"What happens next?" he asked.

I closed my eyes and leaned back against him.

"He takes her other breast in his other hand," I said.

Matt followed suit, pausing to undo the buttons on my blouse. He pushed the fabric aside and lowered the cups of my bra, exposing me completely.

"Um. He plays with her nipples," I continued.

Again, Matt did an excellent job of following directions.

"When does he use his mouth?" he murmured.

"Oh. Hmm. I don't think he did that time. But we can alter the script if you like."

Matt stopped what he was doing and moved to stand in front of me. I pushed my chair back and he reached for my hands, pulling me into a standing position and then lifting me slightly so I was sitting on the table.

"Matt, we eat here," I protested.

"I'm about to."

CHAPTER FIVE

"You watch this ironically, or you really enjoy it?" I asked Matt as we sat in front of yet another reality TV show. I was still enjoying the afterglow of our kitchen encounter as we cuddled on the couch under a warm blanket.

"I enjoy it. Come on, Border Patrol? It's amazing."

I shook my head in wonder. For such an intelligent guy, he had the weirdest taste in television. He would binge the occasional fiction series, but his heart was with the treasure hunters and danger divers. Go figure.

"We're having dinner with Dave and Lynn tonight," I said.

"Okay. That'll be good."

"It's the first time we're going out with them. Think it will be awkward? Your best friend and my best friend. So much combined knowledge at one table," I said.

"Now that would make for a fascinating reality series."

I rolled my eyes at him, then got up to get ready.

*

It was the kind of February evening where your eyelashes froze up the instant you stepped outside. For that reason, I decided we should go to Khyber Pass for dinner, a great little Afghani restaurant in the Plateau area of the city. They had this full dinner special that included an amazing soup with beef and coriander, a pumpkin dish, and then a succulent leg of lamb. It was comfort food to the hilt. Perfect for a frosty night.

"How is it I've lived in this city all my life and never knew about this place?" Dave asked, spearing another forkful of tender lamb.

"Because you weren't hanging around with me," I teased.

"Thank God," Matt muttered.

I looked over at him and smiled.

"Enjoying your meal?" I asked.

"I am. Though I liked it better when you paid for all the meals." Matt grinned.

"Me, too!" Lynn said. "When are you getting that gig back?"

"Relax," I said. "We haven't even been home for a week. Let me settle back in before I go see Sarah."

"We are anxiously waiting," Matt said.

Lynn leaned over and whispered in my ear.

"I dropped something in your pocket when we were hanging up our coats."

I smiled at her.

"Thanks, Lynn," I said. "You're the greatest."

The waiter came to clear the plates and I asked him to give us a few moments before bringing coffee and dessert. We were all on the verge of exploding, and none of us were in a rush to leave. It was nice and cozy in the restaurant. Much less so outside.

"So," Dave asked. "What's on the agenda for the birthday weekend?"

Matt looked at me, appraisingly.

"Well, Allie's got something planned for Friday night that will tie us up until well into Saturday, and then we're having dinner with her parents."

"Dinner with the Styles! An annual birthday tradition," Lynn gushed. "It's been years since

I've been to one of those. Have fun, Matt."

"Should I be nervous?" he asked.

"Not at all," I assured him. "Lynn was the bad influence of my younger years. You are the knight in shining armor. You are perfectly safe."

I leaned over and kissed him.

CHAPTER SIX

When Matt got home from work on Friday evening, I was sitting at the kitchen table dressed only in a light blue lace push-up bra and matching panties. I had a joint ready to go and two glasses of water. Matt walked into the kitchen and stopped dead.

"Whoa. So I guess we're starting the festivities right away?" he asked.

"Go get changed."

I lit the joint as I waited for him. Within two minutes he was back in the kitchen wearing only his boxer briefs.

"I take it this is the appropriate attire for the evening?" he asked.

I laughed and passed him the joint. He took

it and leaned over to kiss me before sitting down.

"So? When are you going to tell me what you've got planned?"

I said nothing but opened my hand, palm up, and revealed two little pink pills. His eyebrows shot up.

"Molly?" he asked.

"Yup."

"Have you ever?"

"Nope. You?"

"Yeah, a few times, but not in over a decade. Wow. Okay."

"I've got Lynn on standby in case anything goes wrong."

Matt laughed.

"This is the birthday gift you wanted? To do Molly with you? I'd do that any day of the week, Allie. I can't believe you didn't let me buy you a gift for this."

"Oh. No. This isn't my gift."

I reached down and pulled a towel out from under the table. I put it down and unwrapped it.

"This is my gift."

It was the apology strap-on he bought me in Amsterdam. He took a long drag on the joint.

"Ah."

He handed me the joint and I stared at him

as he downed his water.

"Go get a sharp knife," he said.

I got up and found a knife, handing it to him and sitting back down.

"Let's just start with half each, why don't we?" he said.

He split the pill and popped his half, taking a swig of my water. Then he passed the glass to me. I swallowed the pill and took a sip.

"Drink all your water," he said.

I did.

"How long?" I asked.

"Oh, you'll know. I hope you don't have anything planned for tomorrow."

"Just dinner with my folks...but it's late."

"Right. Good. Because you are going to feel like shit tomorrow."

"Gee, thanks."

"Let's go lie down on the bed," he said.

"Seriously? Already?"

"Trust me."

He took my hand and I got up and followed him to the bedroom. Trish had taken Loki for the night and she wasn't due to return until about five o'clock the next day. Matt pulled back the duvet and then slid down his boxers. I looked at him.

"Take yours off, too."

I slid out of my panties and unclasped my

bra, letting my breasts fall loose. I was late in my cycle and they were nice and full—perfect sex boobs. Matt was gazing at me with approval in his eyes. I smiled and climbed onto the bed, lying on my back and staring at the ceiling.

"This feels ridiculous," I said.

"Uh, huh," he murmured.

I looked over at him. He was walking around lighting all the candles. When he was done, he shut the overhead light and hooked his phone up to the Bluetooth speaker on the dresser. Rihanna filled the room and the mood shifted. The entire day melted away and suddenly we were in a romantic little love cave. I sat up and waited for him to join me.

"Do we just sit here and wait?" I asked.

He looked at me and rolled his eyes.

"What?" I said. "I've never done this before. In my mind, we should be dancing in a club somewhere."

Matt shrugged.

"That's fun, too. But I have a feeling this will be much more fun."

He glanced nervously over at the strap-on, lying innocently on the night table.

"Well, mostly."

I laughed and flopped onto my back.

"Should we set some ground rules?" I asked.

"Yeah. Don't fuck me up the ass."

"Matt. Come on. If you really don't want to, you know I won't."

"Let's just play it by ear."

We spent the next several minutes talking about our hard limits—of which there were very few. He also warned me that by mutual consent, we could decide to toss those limits out the window. I promised not to hold him to anything. I knew what he was thinking, and while his insecurity was at times charming, it was also infuriating. We both grew quiet and stared up the ceiling for I don't know how long.

"Matt?" I said sometime later.

"Yes?"

"It feels really good when I touch myself."

Matt burst out laughing. When he was able to catch his breath, he turned to me and looked deep into my eyes.

"Yes, I know that. I've watched you do it many times."

"No, I mean, *really* good. Touch me."

He looked down and saw me dragging a finger along my leg and burst out laughing again. He reached over and gently trailed his finger along my cheek. I gasped and closed my eyes.

"Well," he said. "That's that."

As Drake sang to Rihanna about what they could in twenty minutes, Matt got up on his knees and crawled closer to me. He leaned over and kissed me, covering my entire mouth with his own. I thought I was going to pass out. Rather than wrapping my arms around him, I spread them wide, arching my back and offering myself up to him.

"Please. Just touch me," I pleaded.

He pulled away and sat down beside me, cross-legged.

"I guess you've got the faster metabolism," he said. "This is actually kind of funny."

Using his fingertips, he traced a light line from my neck down my arm, setting off every nerve ending along the way. I shivered under his touch.

"Cold?" he asked.

"Not at all. Warm, actually. This feels so good, Matt."

He laughed.

"Wait. It gets better."

"Oh, I don't think it's kicked in yet. I don't feel drunk or anything."

"You won't."

I sat up.

"I won't?"

"Nope. You'll just feel great. Everything will feel great. Life will be good, this music will be heavenly, you'll be blissfully happy. And when I do this—" Matt paused and slid his hand between my legs, causing a small cry to escape my lips. "It's going to feel like the most exquisite thing in the entire world."

I purred.

"Well, that's a new one," he laughed.

He leaned in and kissed me again, easing me back down on the bed. He continued his trail of kisses down my body, causing me to moan and writhe underneath him. It felt fantastic. I felt fantastic. Like a goddess.

"Put something inside me," I said.

He slid his finger in and I closed my eyes in ecstasy as he bent over and licked my nipple before gently taking it in his mouth. I buried my hands in his hair, noticing the feel of each individual strand for the first time. It was so soft, so silky. I got lost in his curls, marveling at the sensation of them against my skin.

"Oh, god, Matt, I want to do everything."

He lifted his head and I saw the look in his eyes had changed, too. He leaned in and kissed me, so slowly, and I savoured the taste of him on my lips. I ran my hands down his back and felt him shudder with pleasure. His skin was like unchartered terrain, something I was discovering for the first time, even though I'd touched him hundreds of times before. It was like we'd previously been two beings, but now we were one.

"Let's be one," I said.

He laughed softly, but by the way he positioned himself over me, he knew exactly what I meant.

"I want you to take me slowly," I said. "I want to feel everything."

"Allie, you're fucking awesome."

He kissed me quickly, then guided himself home, both of us sighing in unison. Then he lifted his leg and closed mine, so that my thighs pressed together. He moved in and out of me two or three times, then pushed his hips into me, going for maximum penetration. Then he stilled, waiting.

I closed my eyes and felt him fill me. I could feel every place his skin touched mine, every inch where we were joined. I lifted my hand and traced his lower lip. He opened his mouth slightly and I slipped my finger inside. As he sucked, he started moving again, increasingly his speed slightly but never breaking a sweat.

I removed my finger from his mouth and wrapped my arms around his waist. As he thrust into me, I slid my hand down to caress his ass and slid my still-wet finger inside. A cry escaped his lips and he stilled.

"Too soon?" I asked.

He shook his head, silent.

"It's okay," he said finally.

He started up again and I slowly moved my finger, getting used to the sensation of being somewhere I had never been before with any man. As I explored, he increased his pace exponentially. Before I knew it, we were bucking hips and he was moaning through his orgasm.

"Fuck me, that was good," he cried as he collapsed on top of me.

I smiled, triumphant.

*

"Wow," he said.

I said nothing. I just lay on my back, staring up and watching the shadows from the candlelight dance across the ceiling.

"You didn't come," he said.

"Don't worry about it. Just keep touching me."

Matt rolled over and ran his hand up and down my arm.

"Not there, you idiot," I said.

He dropped his hand between my legs.

"That's more like it. Why does that feel so good?" I asked.

"Molly."

"I like her," I said as I began to move with his hand. I drew in my breath and brought my hands up to my breasts, caressing myself as if feeling my own skin for the first time. I closed my eyes and pinched both nipples, hearing Matt groan as my orgasm began to build.

"Oh, god. Don't stop," I cried.

I raised my hips off the bed as Matt worked his thumb over my clitoris, making small circles over and over again. I cried out, squeezing my nipples again as I came on his hand, feeling the ripples move through me like never before. Every inch of my body was humming, my skin on fire.

"Holy shit, that felt so good," I said.

"Molly."

"And Matt."

He laughed.

"I just feel so…free. I've never felt like this before. How do I capitalize on this?"

Matt propped himself up on his elbow and studied me.

"What's something you could never imagine yourself doing for me?" he asked.

"Easy. Striptease. I've always been way too self-conscious."

"Hard to believe, but okay. Go ahead."

"What? You want me to do one now?"

"Yes. Why? Don't feel like it?"

I thought about it for a minute. Rihanna was coaxing her rude boy over the speaker. *What the hell.*

"Actually, I do."

Matt smiled and raised his eyebrows at me as I got off the bed and wandered over to the dresser, sifting through my things to find whatever would be most fun to take off. I chose a matching bra and panties set—light pink cotton with lace trim. I slipped them on and walked over to the closet, fingering Matt's crisply-ironed shirts. I pulled one off the hanger and slid into it, doing up the bottom half of the buttons. Just for fun, I grabbed a tie off the rack and fashioned a loose Windsor knot, leaving it to hang between my breasts.

By the time I turned around to face him, Rihanna had left her rude boy behind and was singing about love on the brain. The music was sultry and I moved towards him, swaying my hips to the beat.

Matt sat up in the bed and shuffled his way towards the headboard, propping himself up against some pillows.

"That's what I'm talking about."

His arm drifted down as he watched me, and he took himself in hand, stroking himself absently with one finger but making no motion to get serious. I slowly undid my buttons as

Rihanna pleaded with her man to not to quit loving her. Matt sighed as the shirt fell from my shoulders and dropped to the floor. I ran my hands up my sides, pausing to cup my breasts before shimmying down to the ground as she wailed for a way into his motherfucking heart.

I had never moved like this before in my life. I had no idea if I looked like an idiot, but I had never felt sexier. I was the queen of the fucking world. And the look in Matt's eyes told me he thought so, too. That was all I needed to keep going. I lowered one strap from my shoulder, then the other. I pushed down the fabric of both cups, releasing my breasts.

As I walked towards the bed, I reached behind me to unclasp my bra. Matt reached out to touch me and I slapped his hand away. He laughed and leaned back against the pillows.

"You forgot the tease part of striptease," I said.

"Touche."

I tossed my bra at him and got to work lowering my panties, noticing the sensation of the lace against my skin as it moved down my leg. It sent shivers up my spine. The drug was in full effect by this point and I felt like I was one with the universe, like there was nothing that could possibly go wrong. This was the best moment I had lived, and it was only going to get better.

I climbed onto the bed on all fours, naked except for the tie. Matt leaned forward and grabbed it, pulling me towards him. I landed on his lap, facing him, and leaned forward to kiss him. Kissing Matt had always been a mind-altering experience. He was hands-down the best kisser I'd ever been with. His lips were incredibly soft—gentle yet insistent—and his tongue knew tricks that no tongue should know. But with the added kick of Molly, *holy shit*, Matt's kisses went beyond mind-altering into life-altering territory. I pulled away.

"I have to ask you something," I said.

"What is it?" he asked, running his hands up and down my back.

I had to fight not to get distracted.

"I have wanted to ask you this since the first time we slept together, but I've never had the guts."

He moved his head back to get a better look at me.

"Well, now my curiosity is piqued. What is it?"

"Well," I started. "I just wanted to know, well. I've just never felt this way before, when I was with someone. Having sex with someone. I feel like you know every inch of my body and what it craves at any given moment. I feel so connected to you, so in tune with your moods and desires. You touch me and fireworks go off. I just wanted to know if you feel the same. And if you don't, be gentle. This was hard."

Matt held my face in his hands and looked at me, suddenly very serious.

"Allie. I told you the first night we met it was magic when we touched."

"Yeah, but that was then. Circumstances were different. It was forbidden. That's sexy."

"Allie. I have never in my life felt so close to another human being. If too much time passes and I can't touch you, I'm lost. My body needs yours. I know exactly what you mean because I feel the same."

I leaned over and kissed him.

"I want to fuck you up the ass now," I said.

"Go get the tequila."

I flew from the bedroom to fetch the bottle and a shot glass before he had a chance to change his mind. I didn't even stop to consider the implications of mixing alcohol with the MDMA. When I returned to the bedroom, I found Matt sitting on the bed, cross-legged, stroking the inside of his calves.

"Feels good, huh?" I asked.

"It really fucking does."

I handed him the bottle and glass, and he

proceeded to pour himself a shot, then two, and then a third. While he was pouring the fourth, I picked up the strap-on and fit it into place. I turned to look at myself in the mirror.

"Wow," I said. "I suddenly understand why you men walk around feeling so powerful all the time."

Matt groaned and rolled his eyes. I turned and looked at him.

"Close your eyes," I said.

I walked over to the bed and knelt, kissing him softly on the mouth. He reached out blindly and found my face, holding my chin while I deepened the kiss. I ran my hands over his shoulders, then quietly climbed onto the bed. I reached over and picked up the lube.

"Is that the lube I hear? Please use the entire bottle," Matt said.

I laughed and ran my hands over his back and his ass, gently guiding him into position. I got behind him and reached around him to take him in my hand, stroking him until he grew hard. I kept my other hand on his ass and slowly slid my finger in. He grunted but didn't ask me to stop.

I pulled my hand away and took hold of the strap-on, guiding it towards him. I could not believe I was actually doing it, but somehow, through the fog of the drug, it seemed like the most natural thing in the world. Slowly, I slid into him and I heard him take in a sharp breath. I stilled.

"It's okay," he said.

I continued to move slowly, taking my time with this completely new sensation for both of us. I wished I'd had the double-header (ha!) Maja had in Amsterdam—I'm pretty sure I could've gotten off in two minutes flat. As I felt Matt relax, I put both my hands on his hips and pushed in a little deeper. I was so completely turned on, and I only hoped it wasn't horrible for Matt.

"You're doing great, baby." I said.

He grunted in reply. I reached back around and took him in hand, stroking him and squeezing lightly, while I continued to penetrate him from behind.

"Okay!" he said. "You're in. We did it."

I stilled again.

"You want me to pull out? You want me to stop?"

He was silent for a moment.

"No."

CHAPTER SEVEN

"Allie?"

"Yeah?"

"Someone's knocking at the door."

I opened my eyes and reached over to pick up my phone. It was 11 o'clock. We had both been fast asleep.

"It must be Trish, with Loki," I said.

"You should get that, then."

"It's my birthday," I reasoned.

Matt sighed and pulled back the covers as he got up. He pulled on his pajama bottoms and reached for a shirt.

"No," I said. "No shirt. I'm showing you off."

He smirked at me and padded out of the

room.

I lay in bed, staring at the ceiling, listening to him walk down the hallway and work the lock on the door. I felt truly shitty. I'm sure Matt did, as well. The aftereffects of Molly. And tequila. And maybe a little bit of pot in there somewhere. Definitely too old for that shit.

I heard muffled voices in the hallway, and then Matt's footsteps approaching. He shuffled into the bedroom, scratching his head, and gave me a funny look.

"What's up?" I asked. "Something wrong with Loki?"

"It's not Trish," he said. "It's Josh."

I sat up fast, then grimaced at the pain in my head.

"Yeah, I got that, too," Matt said.

"I don't want to see Josh."

"Well—"

"Just tell him to go," I whispered. "Tell him I'm not here."

He came over and sat down on the bed. He took my hand and kissed my palm.

"Please," he said. "Just go talk to him."

I took my hand back and slid out of bed. I pulled on a pair of sweats and a T-shirt and walked to the door, shooting him one last look before going into the hallway.

Josh was standing inside the apartment, the

door closed. He looked at me, slightly pained, then readjusted his expression. He was holding a box.

"Happy birthday, Allie."

I didn't need to look inside to know what it contained. It was a Black Forest cake, a joke tradition between us on our birthdays.

"Josh," I said.

"Please. Just let me speak."

He looked around and put the cake down on the entryway table. Then he looked at me, all wide-eyed and puppy-like. My heart melted just a bit. Out of nostalgia, I was sure.

"What is it?"

"When I saw you, all those months ago, well, it did something to me. It made me realize what an idiot I'd been. You were the best thing that ever happened to me and I let you just slip away. All because I was too scared to get married. But Allie, you didn't understand. Your parents are still so happy together. Mine split when I was eight. It was awful. But now I see I was wrong. I just want another chance."

I backed away from him as he spoke. When he was done, I just shook my head sadly.

"Josh," I said. "It's too late. I'm sorry. I met someone. And I really like him. It's just too late."

"But, Allie-"

"Josh. You'll find someone, too. I know you will. Now that you're open to it, you will. But please, just go. I thank you for the gesture, but it's misplaced. I'm sorry."

I turned at a slight noise behind me and saw Matt standing in the doorway of the bedroom, now wearing a shirt. He raised an eyebrow, wanting to make sure I had everything under control. I smiled and gave him a slight nod. He retreated into the bedroom.

I turned back to Josh.

"Just go."

*

I locked the front door and walked back to the bedroom. Matt was sitting on the bed.

"Happy birthday?" he said.

I laughed.

"What a way to start the year. Christ."

I sat down next to him. We were silent for a moment, and then I turned to him and kissed him on the mouth. I put my hand on his cheek and used my tongue to gently part his lips. He obliged and kissed me deeply.

"There's only you," I whispered.

Matt sighed and looked down.

"What?" I asked, already impatient.

It was definitely the hangover.

"You told him it was too late," Matt said.

"It *is* too late."

"You didn't tell him you didn't love him anymore. You said it was too late."

I paused. He was right.

"Matt. It's my birthday. And I don't want to talk about this anymore. Can we please put a pin in it until tomorrow?"

"You think we can do that?" he asked.

"I do. We must. We're having a late dinner with my parents tonight," I reminded him.

"Right. Shit. Okay."

He got up off the bed and paced for a bit.

"Really?" I asked. "You're trying to figure out how to ignore this issue for one day?"

"Yes. I am. This is weighing on me, Allie."

I stood up and peeled off my clothes. I climbed onto the bed and got on all fours. I looked back at him over my shoulder.

"Grab the tequila," I said. "You kept your word, I'm going to keep mine."

Matt stopped dead in his tracks. And then he slowly shook his head.

"No. I mean, yes, of course yes, but no. Not now. Not when I'm feeling this crappy and we're having dinner with your parents."

"Well, you can at least come fuck me, then."

He pulled the drawstring on his waist and came towards me.

"Yes, I can definitely do that."

He stepped out his pajama bottoms and pulled his shirt over his head in that sexy way guys do. He took himself in hand, slowly stroking to bring himself to full attention. I loved when he touched himself, holding his length in his strong hand. It was so incredibly erotic, watching him grow hard like that. My breath quickened as he looked at me, my nipples hardening under his gaze.

"Touch yourself," he said.

I slid one hand between my legs, slipping one finger inside as I closed my eyes.

"Are you wet?" he asked.

"I am so wet, Matt. Come fuck me."

He grabbed my hips, and in one motion, thrust his full length inside of me. I gasped and grabbed hold of the duvet to ground myself. He fucked me hard and fast, both of us coming within twenty strokes. We fell exhausted onto the bed and passed out again for another three hours.

CHAPTER EIGHT

We stood at the front of the restaurant, waiting to be seated by the maitre d'. My parents had a penchant for nice steakhouses and that night had been no exception. It was my birthday, which meant reasonably it should've been my pick, but I liked steak so I never complained. It was all my father would eat in restaurants, anyway. Anything else could "just as easily be made at home." Not by him, of course.

I had a pretty good relationship with my parents. My mother and I were close while I was growing up, and we remained in pretty constant contact. My parents had been married for forty years, and all evidence pointed to the fact that they were happy. They liked Josh a lot, so I was a little nervous about introducing them to Matt, but he was such a great guy I didn't see how it could go wrong.

"Do you think they're here already?" Matt asked, looking a little nervous.

"Don't be nervous," I said. "They're nice people."

"I'm fucking their daughter. Of course, I'm nervous."

On cue, the maitre d' appeared. After trying to suppress a grin, he led us to the table where my parents were, in fact, waiting. Out of the corner of my eye, I saw the maitre d' give Matt a supportive clap on the shoulder. My dad stood as I approached. I immediately went over and hugged him, then leaned down to kiss my mom on the cheek.

"Mom, Dad, this is Matt."

I stood back to let them shake hands and took the opportunity to imagine what it would be like to see my parents through a stranger's eyes. My dad was in his late fifties, growing a bit of a belly but still in good overall shape. My mom was 55, vibrant, and full of energy. They were both down-to-earth people, zero pretenses about them.

Introductions done and hands shaken, we all sat and the waiter came over to take our drink orders. *Smart server.* I mentally made a note to throw in some extra for his tip. That was a bit of a weak spot with my dad.

"It's great to finally meet you," Matt said.

"We've heard quite a bit about you, as well," my mom said. "Interesting work you do."

Matt gave a nervous laugh.

"Well, the work's not as interesting as the opportunities it affords me."

My dad nodded appreciatively.

"You like to travel?"

"I do," Matt said. "And getting to do it on someone else's dime is even better."

We all laughed at that.

"You want to order for us, Allison?" my mother asked.

"No, Mom. I trust everyone knows what they want to eat."

"Allison, huh? You said no one calls you that," Matt said, smiling.

I rolled my eyes at him.

We spent the rest of the meal catching up, Matt and I filling them in on (most of) our adventures in Amsterdam and my folks recounting their activities of the past few months. It was an exceedingly pleasant evening, and I was just thinking about how well things were going when my father pulled one of his classic moves.

"So? Hear from Josh ever?" he asked.

Everyone at the table went silent, except Matt, who put down his fork and looked at my dad.

"Actually," Matt said. "He showed up at the apartment this morning with a birthday cake for your daughter."

My dad turned beet red.

"Not the answer you were expecting, Dad?" I asked, laughing.

"Well," my mother huffed, "I hope you don't make the same foolish mistakes he made, Matt."

"Mother!" I cried. "We've been dating for five months."

"You're living together."

"Out of convenience!" I said.

My mother just shook her head. I sighed.

"Hey. Are we all okay here? You like Matt, yes?"

Matt looked suitably embarrassed as my parents sheepishly nodded their heads.

"Okay, then let's just drop this. It's my birthday."

I slunk down a little in my chair as I saw the waiters approaching with the restaurant's signature vanilla-peach birthday cake. I braced myself for the singing of *Happy Birthday* and then reluctantly set about slicing up the cake. If there was one thing in this world I wished I didn't have to share, it was Gibby's birthday cake.

My mom leaned over in her seat and whispered in my ear.

"I want to hear more about this morning's visit," she said.

I gave her a slight nod and passed her a plate.

*

Later that night, I was peeling off my clothes while Matt walked around the bedroom, lighting the random candles I'd had out forever but never used. I smiled to myself, wondering what kind of escapades he had in mind and whether I had the energy for them. I was still suffering from the aftereffects of the long night before.

"That went well, didn't it?" I asked.

"It did," he said. "Or at least I thought so. I liked your parents."

"They definitely liked you. I can tell."

Matt walked over to me as he unbuttoned his shirt.

"Let me do that," I said.

I met him halfway and removed his hands, taking over the task myself. I leaned over to kiss the exposed parts of his chest as I worked and smiled as I heard him sigh. He wrapped his arms around me loosely, resting them on my hips.

"Hey," he said softly. I looked up.

He kissed me then, and everything melted away. It was so gentle and full of tenderness that for a ridiculous moment I thought I might cry. I slid my hands under his shirt and held him close. I was naked at this point, and I felt him grow hard as my breasts pressed up against his bare chest.

"You're ready for me," I smiled at him.

"You ready for me?" he asked.

"Always."

He slid one arm below my ass and lifted me off the ground, carrying me, bride-like, over to the bed. He lay me down and paused to pull off his pants. Then he climbed up, positioning himself over me and resting his weight on his elbows.

He kissed me again, and this time I responded by pressing my hips up against his. He moved down, kissing my jaw and my neck, then coming back up to nibble on my ear. I snaked my arms around his waist, grasping his ass in my hands and pulling him in towards me. He continued to take his time, kissing me slowly, then dipping to take one nipple in his mouth.

I moaned, sinking into the bed and getting swept up in pure sensation. He moved to my other breast, taking it in his mouth and gently sucking, causing waves of desire to spread through my body.

"Matt…"

He brought his head up and kissed me on the mouth, biting my lower lip gently. As I raised my hips in response, I felt him slide into me, slow and gentle. The feeling was exquisite. It was the most vanilla sex we'd had in ages—missionary-style, on the bed, at night—yet it was so intense and erotic. I couldn't stop my hands from moving over his body, caressing his back and his ass and he moved inside me.

"I want you to come, Allie."

"Matt-"

"Shhh," he said.

He adjusted his position slightly—once, twice—until I felt contact between him and my sweet spot. I gasped and he pulled back a little, smiling.

"Have I got it, then?" he asked.

I nodded, speechless. He closed his eyes and picked up speed, just a little, allowing me time to catch up. Tiny little rockets started going off in my head as my body built towards orgasm. A cry escaped, and that was Matt's cue to drive it home. He leaned in and planted one last kiss on my mouth, then thrust into to me until I came, loudly, wrapping my legs around his waist and holding him tightly in my arms.

I felt his release quickly follow my own, and I slowly let my legs fall back to the bed. He propped himself up and brushed the hair out of my eyes. I gazed at him.

"You just made love to me," I said.

He laughed.

"No," I said. "I mean, you didn't fuck me. You made love to me. You haven't done that since the first time we were together."

His expression grew serious.

"Allie. I told you the other day. I love you."

The shock must have been apparent in my eyes, because he climbed off of me and sat on the bed, taking one of my hands in his. He brought it up to his lips and kissed it, stroking my knuckles with his thumb.

"I thought that was a casual response to some great sex," I said.

"No. I meant it."

I sat up and took his face in my hands. I leaned over and kissed him.

"I love you, too, Matt."

"Happy birthday."

CHAPTER NINE

By Thursday I knew I'd have to go and see Sarah, my editor at the paper. It wasn't that I didn't want to go back to reviewing restaurants, it was just that I was having so much fun writing the erotica. But I knew it was smart to rake in the cash while I could, and having my meals covered was a great way to do that. Plus, it kept my writing skills sharp. I just had to ensure I wasn't describing food in erotic terms.

"Allie Styles," she said as I walked into her office. "Shut the door."

I closed the door behind me and took a seat across from her.

"Or," she said. "Should I call you Temple

Fraser? Holy shit, you can write, girl."

I smiled.

"Thank you. And THANK you."

"I wasn't sure I'd see you again in my office. You saying you're ready to come back?"

"I am."

"Okay, then. My current critic has six weeks left on her contract. I will not renew."

I shifted, uncomfortable.

"What's wrong, Allie?"

"Well, it's just that I might be going away again."

"Allie. Figure this out, then come see me."

"You're right, I'm sorry."

"Don't apologize. I'm always happy to see you. Also, I kinda wanted to ask, the Christmas market—?"

I raised my eyebrows and walked out the door.

*

I was lying on the living room floor, trying to alleviate a sore back from sitting at the computer all day, when Matt came home from work.

"Waiting for me?" he asked, hopeful.

"No. Trying to work out a kink."

"Like I said, waiting for me?"

I laughed, then grimaced at the spasm that went through my back.

"There are all kinds of weird side effects to your job," he marveled.

He made his way into the kitchen and I heard him rummaging around in the fridge for a snack.

"How'd it go with Sarah?" he called.

I waited until he came back into the living room, not wanting to risk whatever agony yelling might bring.

"Not great. I mean, she was happy to see me, but as I sat there, I realized I can't take that job back if I'm leaving again soon."

Matt sat down on the floor next to me, set down the box, and started rolling a joint.

"Have you tried this for your back?"

"No, actually. Didn't even think of it."

We sat quietly for a moment. Matt finished rolling and sparked up. He took a few tokes, then passed it to me.

"When are we leaving anyway?" I asked. "Any news on that front?"

Matt was silent.

"Matt? What's going on?"

"Yes, there's news. I leave next week. And I'm not one hundred percent sure you should come with me."

"WHAT?"

So much for not yelling. I struggled to sit up, propping myself up against the couch.

"What the fuck are you talking about?"

"Just listen to me."

He gave me a moment to work through my shock and impulsive anger, then continued.

"I can't stop thinking about Josh, and what happened between the two of you. I love you, Allie, there's no secret there. And I know you love me. This isn't about that. I know how amazing we are together. But we both need to be sure that you're done with Josh. He was too late—that thought keeps haunting me. And I know you've thought about it, too."

"Matt, you're being crazy."

"No, I'm not. Think about it. You can come join me anytime. And I hope you will. But I, we, need you to take the time with him and sort through your feelings."

"Why are you such a fucking grownup?" I asked him, angry.

He just smiled.

"You are, too. You know it. Just think about it. You'll see I'm right."

"Well, I don't feel like being a grownup right now," I said.

"You want me to sleep on the couch?"

"You still paying rent at Dave's?"

Matt stopped smiling and looked at me.

"You serious?"

"Yes," I said.

He stood up.

"All right, then. I can respect that. I love you, Allie. Think about this. Call me when you're ready."

*

Twenty minutes later, I was back in my previous position flat on my back when my cell phone rang.

"Why is Matt here? Why is he sleeping here? What the fuck is going on?"

Lynn, on the other end of the phone, was clearly upset. I just didn't know if she was upset for me or if Matt had somehow thrown a monkey wrench in her own plans.

"Lynn, calm down. We just had a disagreement, and I didn't want to share a bed with him angry. That's all. Did I ruin your plans?"

"No, of course not. Do you need me to come over?"

"No," I laughed. "I need you to spy for me."

"Right. I got you."

I pulled myself up off the floor and walked to the kitchen. I shut down my laptop and opened the fridge, staring blindly for a moment before pulling out a mason jar of iced tea. Loki came up and nuzzled my knee. I scratched her head and we both retreated to the bedroom for the night.

CHAPTER TEN

I woke the next morning fairly early but didn't get out of bed. I lay there for an undetermined amount of time, just staring out the window. Loki was content to lie beside me, curled up with every inch of her back in direct contact with my body.

I thought about my conversation with Matt and for the first time wondered if he had a point. Things hadn't ended properly with Josh. That was no secret. And maybe there were unresolved feelings there. But I also knew what I felt for Matt. What would it serve for me to move backwards?

Whatever I thought, clearly Matt thought differently. He was almost pushing for me to get back together with Josh. I had to admit, I could see it from his point of view. If he was going to invest emotionally in me, he wanted to be sure I was fully available.

My phone buzzed and I picked it up off the night table to check my texts.

Hey.

I smiled to myself. I could almost hear the sheepish tone in Matt's voice.

Hey, yourself.

I miss you.

Come home.

Can we discuss this calmly?

Maybe.

My phone rang.

"What?" I said.

"Just tell me we can sit down and have a rational conversation about this. I don't want to lose you, Allie. I want to be secure in knowing I have you."

"How can anyone ever be secure?" I asked.

He sighed.

"Fine. We'll discuss it. Come home."

I hung up the phone and rolled out of bed. My back was still sore, but it would be manageable. I got up and pulled on some pajamas. Loki reluctantly got off the bed and followed me into the kitchen. I boiled the water for tea and popped a bagel into the toaster, then turned back and went to the bathroom.

I was sitting at the table, just finishing off my breakfast when I heard Matt's key turn in the lock. I got up to greet him at the door. He smiled when he saw me and dropped his bag.

"Let's not do that again," he said.

"Well that's up to you, isn't it?" I asked.

He tensed, so I walked over to him and put my arms around his waist. I tilted my head up for a kiss. He just looked at me.

"Just kiss me," I said.

"We're not having sex."

"I don't want to have sex. I just want you to kiss me."

He took my face in his hands and leaned down. His mouth covered mine and I closed my eyes. I was home. I was careful to keep my distance and not inadvertently attempt to seduce him in any way. He needed to know my word was golden. When he pulled back, I opened my eyes and looked at him.

"That's better," I said.

I released him and turned back into the apartment. I made my way to the living room and sat down on the couch. He followed and sat down next to me. I moved over a bit and swung my feet up into his lap. He looked at me, puzzled.

"Nothing can be so bad if you're rubbing my

feet," I explained.

He laughed and took one of my feet in hand, settling himself into the couch. He began what can only be described as a mind-blowing foot massage.

"Allie. I think you should call him. See him. Even if it's just once. And it shouldn't be while I'm here. I cloud your vision. I know that because I can't fucking think clearly when you're around."

"That's called testosterone," I interjected.

"Allie. Fuck. Just hear me out. I am leaving this week—something I meant to discuss with you yesterday, but, well, you were here. I don't think I need to explain. But I think I should go, and you should stay. You should see Josh. You should work this out, for his sake and yours. I will be waiting for you if you come."

"If I come?"

"Well—"

"And when do you leave?" I asked.

"In five days."

"On Wednesday?"

"Yes."

"And are we supposed to have sex until then? With both of us knowing I'm going on a date with my ex next week?" I asked, incredulous.

"Well, I hadn't really thought that part out. I

want to stay here. Last night was horrible. Lynn and Dave are really fucking loud."

I shot him a look.

"But more so," he continued. "I hated knowing you were so close and I wasn't with you. You don't want to have sex, we won't have sex. But I want to stay."

"Fine."

*

The mood was tense as Matt started packing for his trip. He had no idea how long he'd be gone. He grew quiet when I offered to bring some of his stuff when I joined him. Rather than picking a fight, I dropped it. I knew this was hard on him, too.

We spent most of the weekend together, though he did take off to spend some time with Dave. Lynn and I used that time to catch up and see a movie. It had been a while since we'd had a boy-free afternoon together and we kept the conversation to work, life, and strictly away from both Matt and Dave.

We shared a bed, but good to his word Matt didn't make a move on me. I lay there for two nights, staring at the wall and wondering if I should reach out to him.

On Monday morning, as he was getting

ready to go into the office and pack up his things, he turned to me before leaving the kitchen. I put down my tea and looked up at him.

"I'm having dinner with my family tomorrow night. They want to see me before I go. Will you come?" he asked.

I didn't hesitate.

"Of course I'll come. I would love to meet your family."

He smiled, relieved, and walked down the hall towards the door.

After he left, I sat there, thinking about the significance of this dinner. It meant he still hoped I'd join him. Why else would he have wanted to introduce me to his parents? But then why insist I see Josh? Again, it came back, at least in my mind, to him wanting to be sure I wouldn't have a change of heart later down the road. I shook my head at how ridiculous it all was, but also determined to be softer towards him. He was leaving after all.

When he came home that night, I had dinner ready. It was rare that I cooked, but I made him a nice, rich boeuf bourguignon, a lovely stew made with red wine and tender beef. We ate in the kitchen, sharing the remnants of the burgundy wine I used for dinner. He relaxed when he saw I had changed my attitude, and by the end of the meal had even warmed up.

"Getting excited?" I asked.

"Trepidatious," he said. "Still not a hundred percent sure what awaits me. Although I do know what I'm leaving behind."

I opened my mouth to tell him that was his choice, but remembered the promise I'd made to myself to be kinder and closed it again. I smiled instead and got up to clear the dishes. I placed them in the sink and then took the entire pot of stew and put it in the fridge. Tupperware be damned. I turned to him.

"Let's go sit in the living room. Bring the wine."

He got up and did as told, following me, and we both settled in on the couch. He passed me my glass and I took a deep sip before putting it down on the coffee table.

"Two more nights, huh?" I asked.

He nodded.

"It would be a shame to waste those."

He closed his eyes and all remaining traces of tension left his face.

"Thank you, Lord," he whispered.

I picked up his hand and kissed each of his fingertips before taking his index finger into my mouth. He groaned and opened his eyes.

"Trust me, Allie, I don't need further persuasion."

I gently put down his hand and got up from the couch. I walked over to the bookshelf and turned back towards him.

"What are you doing?" he asked, suspicious.

I reached up to one of the higher shelves and grabbed hold of my DSLR. I turned back towards him and placed the camera on the coffee table. I sat back down.

"I was thinking about a little going-away present," I said.

He exhaled slowly.

"You serious?" he asked.

"Yup."

He looked down, then over at me, almost embarrassed.

"What is it?" I asked.

He cleared his throat and pulled out his phone.

"I've got a shot list."

I burst out laughing.

"Let's hear it."

He unlocked his phone and found his list. Turning just the slightest shade of red, he read to me.

"Naked, in one of my button-downs."

"Done."

"Naked."

"Assumed. Next."

"Naked and touching yourself?"

"Fine."

There was silence. I glanced over and saw he had turned a slightly deeper shade of red.

"Go ahead," I said. "You're not going to shock me."

"Shaving yourself?" he whispered, so softly I barely heard him.

"Huh," I said. "You prefer me bare? Why didn't you ever say anything?"

"No, I don't. It's not that. I just think, well, it would be really hot to watch you shave."

I tilted my head and looked at him, then shrugged.

"Okay. That it?"

"One more."

"Well?"

He cleared his throat again.

"I want a picture of you sucking my cock."

"MATTHEW!"

He shrunk back a little but held his ground.

"I would never show it to anyone, I swear. You can ask me to delete it whenever you want. But, fuck, Allie. It would be so hot."

I sighed.

"I'll think about it."

I got up and started walking towards the bedroom.

"Where are you going?" Matt asked.

I turned back to look at him, flashing a smile.

"To find a button-down."

He grinned from ear-to-ear and leaned over to pick up the camera. As I turned into the bedroom, he was already taking practice shots.

I walked over to the closet and opted for a plain white shirt. I slowly took off my clothes, suddenly wishing I'd had more wine, or at least smoked a joint. I'd never done this before. I'd never trusted anyone enough—not even Josh. Though Josh would never have asked. And Josh never got off on watching me touch myself like Matt did. He felt he should always be the one to make me come. And I don't think he ever jerked off in front of me. I shook my head, thinking about it.

Once naked, I pulled Matt's shirt off the hanger and slid it on. I didn't bother with the buttons. I let my fingers graze the sides of my breasts as I straightened the fabric around me. It was perfectly ironed, of course, because... well, Matt. I smiled to myself and closed the door to look at myself in the full-length mirror.

When I did, I saw Matt reflected back at me, standing in the doorway. He slowly brought the camera up to his eye and began shooting me. I turned to look at him over my shoulder and smiled. I looked back in the mirror, fixed my hair and straightened my collar, then walked towards the bed.

I climbed on and got on my knees, facing Matt.

"What do you want me to do?" I asked.

He hadn't stopped shooting since he walked in the door. Now he lowered the camera and looked at me, lust in his eyes.

"Touch your tits," he said.

"We're jumping ahead of schedule here, aren't we?"

"Shut up."

I gave him a little salute, then dropped my hand to my neck. From there, I let my fingers slowly trail downward, towards my left breast. He brought the camera up again and continued taking pictures, more slowly now. I rubbed my breast, licking my lips and staring at the camera. It was already getting difficult to breathe.

"You ever done this before?" I asked.

"No. You?"

"No."

"What do you think?" he asked.

"It's really fucking hot."

I dropped my hand between my legs and slid two fingers inside, using my thumb to rub my clitoris. I brought my other hand back up to my breast and I heard Matt groan.

"Do that thing, Allie, with your palm."

I opened my eyes and smiled at him. I loved

this man. I slid my fingers out and, with a flat palm, began to rub myself slowly, rocking my hips back and forth into my hand. Matt got down on his knees and kept shooting. I let go of my breast and reached over to run my hand through his hair. He put down the camera and climbed onto the bed. He undid the buckle on his belt while I unbuttoned his shirt. Together we lowered his pants and I got down on all fours to take him in my mouth.

He sighed and buried his hands in my hair. I supported myself on one arm as I used my other hand to cup his balls, gently rolling and squeezing as I took him deeper into my mouth. I felt him start to constrict and pulled away.

"What are you doing?" he asked, his voice thick.

"Get the camera."

His eyes rolled up into his head. I thought he was going to pass out. He reached over and picked up the camera. I then took him in my hand, and holding his shaft, gently swirled my tongue around his tip. I heard him moan and looked up just in time for him to snap a picture. *That'll be a keeper*.

I got back to my work and heard the camera fall back to the bed. Matt put his hands on my face and gently pulled me away. He raised me back up onto my knees and pulled me in close, kissing me deeply.

"You make every dream come true," he whispered.

"How do you want me?"

"Just like this."

He reached down and guided himself into me, then wrapped his arms around me and took hold of my ass. We moved together, on our knees, and it was the perfect position to create maximum friction for me. I let a soft moan escape as I took hold of Matt's shoulders, getting that internal thrill at the feel of his muscles beneath my fingertips. Matt took one hand off my ass to reach down between us and rub my sweet spot, ensuring I wouldn't get left behind. I kissed him, moving my hands from his shoulders to his cheeks, holding him close as he fucked me into oblivion.

The orgasm erupted between my legs, quickly fanning out to all my extremities. I wrapped my arms around him, no longer able to support myself on my knees, and collapsed against him. He held onto my ass and continued to thrust until he came, calling out my name as he ran his hands up and down my back.

*

"You didn't tell me we were going to your parents' *house* for dinner."

We had just pulled up outside a modest but elegant home in Hampstead, an upper-class area of the city. When Matt invited me to dinner, I just assumed it would be a restaurant. Neutral ground. This was not neutral ground.

"Don't worry," he said. "I brought flowers."

"That's not the point."

"They're sweet. You'll love them. Don't worry."

I looked around as I got out of the car. Though not Jewish myself, I grew up with a lot of Jewish friends. Many of their parents lived in Hampstead, so I knew the area quite well. In fact, I recognized a man across the street, shoveling his walk, as the father of a kid I used to hang out with after school.

Matt led me up the front steps and gave the bell a polite ring before opening the door and walking in.

"Mom? Dad?"

A beautiful woman in her late twenties came down the stairs, smiling at Matt. She looked just like him, but the ultra-feminine version. Same curly hair, same sea-green eyes. I liked her right away.

"Becky!"

Matt took the stairs two at a time, meeting

his sister halfway and giving her a big hug. She laughed and looked over his shoulder at me.

"Is this Allie?"

I smiled shyly.

"It is," Matt said. "Becky, Allie. Allie, Becky."

Becky made her way down the rest of the staircase and came over to shake my hand. She was pure joy and light and I was beginning to get a sense of what it was like growing up in the Goldberg household. Without even meeting his parents, I knew Becky was the glue that kept this family together.

"It's great to meet you," I said. "I've heard so much about you."

"Same!" she laughed.

At that moment, Matt's parents came out of the kitchen and walked towards us. They looked to be in their late fifties or early sixties. His dad was on the heavy side but had the build of an ex-football player. His mom was lovely. She was beautiful, warm, and kind-looking. I felt like I was in a Hallmark movie.

Matt made introductions, but it was barely necessary. His parents were welcoming and we all retreated to the living room for drinks. There was even Tanqueray.

"Matt hasn't brought home a girlfriend in over ten years!" Becky said gleefully.

"Becky," Matt said.

"But it's true. This is exciting."

Matt rolled his eyes.

The living room looked like it was straight out of the nineties. The furniture had clearly been handed down from another generation, but it was well cared for and suited the surroundings. Everyone else took a seat, but I couldn't resist walking around and looking at all the old family photos. When Matt saw what I was up to, he jumped up and came to join me.

"So Matt tells us you're a food critic," Mrs. Goldberg said.

"Yes. I am. I love it. I get to eat everywhere."

"Maybe you can put some weight on my son," she said.

"Mom," Matt said, then turned to me. "You have to understand Jewish mothers."

"Oh, I do," I assured him.

Josh's mother had been the stereotypical Jewish mother—complete with attachment issues to her son. I turned to Mrs. Goldberg.

"Your son is perfect," I said.

She smiled approvingly.

I walked slowly along the framed photos on the bookshelves, delighting in the pictures of Matt as a boy—playing in the ocean, eating ice cream with his sister. Along the walls were his official school portraits, from kindergarten right up to university convocation. I stopped at that photo, staring at the image of him in cap and gown. My knees went weak.

"What?" he asked.

"Swoon," I replied.

He put his arm around my waist, gave me a slight squeeze, and led me to the couch. I couldn't help but notice the smile that passed between his parents.

The evening went off without a hitch. I aced every test, although I had the sense it wouldn't have been too difficult. Matt's family was clearly thrilled to see him so happy. We ate, drank some more, and eventually stumbled home at around ten o'clock.

"So," I said, closing the apartment door behind me. "You wanted to see me shave?"

"I'll get the camera."

*

Wednesday morning, I stood by the front door of the apartment, waiting for Matt to finish saying goodbye to Loki in the bedroom. She refused to budge, knowing something unpleasant was up.

"You coming?" I called.

"Give me a minute."

I started throwing Matt's bags out into the

hallway and he appeared by my side, grabbing me around the waist for a kiss.

"I will miss you," he said.

"I'll be there soon," I said.

He grabbed a jacket off the hook in the hall and we left the apartment together for the last time. Neither of us knew when he'd be back.

On the drive to the airport, we were both a little lost for conversation.

"It went well last night with my parents, don't you think?" he asked.

"I do. I really liked them. They're great."

"I think they really liked you, too."

"I think they'd like anyone willing to take in your raggedy ass."

Matt laughed. I pulled up outside the departure terminal. Once again, I opted not to go in with him. Last time it was because I didn't know him well enough. This time it was because I knew him too well. I couldn't bear the thought of him leaving, but if he needed me to work things out with Josh to feel secure, I would do that for him. I would have done anything for him.

I turned the off the car. We looked at each other.

"So this is it," he said.

"This is it."

We both got out of the car and unloaded his

bags. He went for a cart and I stood there, watching him. I had the feeling that if we stayed together, I'd spend a lot of time watching him walk away. Or, maybe I'd be going with him. I understood why it had been so many years since his last relationship. It must have been incredibly difficult to always be putting his life on hold. But if I went with him, his traveling could *become* our life—no more putting things on hold.

Matt came back and piled his bags onto the cart. He gathered me up in his arms and I buried my head in his chest, breathing in deeply and savouring the scent. It was a cold March day but his body, as always, was like a walking furnace. I always ran cold. Another way we were perfect for each other.

He pulled back and raised my face towards his as he leaned down to kiss me. I closed my eyes and held him close, never wanting to let him go. I have no idea how long we stood there, but when we finally came up for air, he had the saddest look in his eyes.

"I love you, Allie Styles."

"I love you, Matt Goldberg."

He gathered up his stuff, grabbed hold of his cart, and made his way into the terminal.

CHAPTER ELEVEN

It took me a week after Matt left to pick up the phone and call Josh. It also took a glass of wine and a joint, but that was beside the point. He picked up before the first ring.

"Allie?"

"It's me."

"How are you? What's up?"

He sounded eager, yet reserved. Tentative. Not a word I'd ever have ascribed to Josh. Josh was confident, successful, driven.

"Well, I was wondering if you'd want to grab some dinner."

"I'd love that, but I'm out of town at the moment. I'll be back in about two weeks. Can I call you then?" he asked.

"Sure."

"Allie?"

"Yes?"

"It's really great to hear from you."

My heart warmed. I couldn't help it. *Josh.*

Another two weeks. By the time I saw Josh, Matt would have been gone a month. I had thought I'd follow behind him by a couple of days, a week tops. Suddenly, I was looking at a month. It was cruel. I picked up my phone again, checking the time. Five o'clock here, so midnight for Matt.

Hey. You up?

I sat and waited for a few minutes, about to give up, when the phone buzzed.

Yeah. How are you?

I miss you.

Same…Have you seen Josh?

No. I finally got in touch, but he's out of town. Matt, I won't see him for another two weeks. You sure about this?

Positive.

I was sitting on the couch, dressed only in a pair of sweats and a V-neck T-shirt. I smiled to myself, pulled aside my collar, and snapped a picture of my boob for him. I sent it through.

Oh, Allie. I do love you.

You're so weird.

I put down the phone and got up to make

dinner.

*

Lynn and I were sitting in a Juliette and Chocolat in the Monkland village, enjoying a delicious hot chocolate and watching the snow melt outside. It was late March and the winter had been brutal. We were both eager for spring and slightly bitter that we were drinking hot chocolate instead of milkshakes.

"How's the writing going?" Lynn asked.

"Okay," I said. "I've still got some material, but I'm starting to run a little dry…"

Lynn laughed.

"Dave says Matt's working hard."

"He is. I barely get to speak to him. The time difference really screws with us, too. I miss him."

"You're seeing Josh tomorrow, right?"

"Yeah."

"Nervous?"

"Hell, yes."

We sat silently, drinking and people-watching.

"I really don't want to do this, Lynn."

"I get it, Allie. But I see Matt's side, too. It's pretty crazy that this is his idea, though. That's one hell of a guy you found there."

I smiled.

"I know."

"Dave thinks the whole thing is insane. He says Matt hasn't had a girlfriend in over a decade, that you're the perfect woman for him, and then he goes and throws it all away. His theory is that Matt is just self-sabotaging. For some reason, he doesn't think he's worthy of you, so he's preemptively taking care of it."

"What?" I said. "That's nuts. Matt said that?"

"No! That's just Dave's theory."

"Dave's theory is ass," I said.

Lynn laughed.

"Whatever," I said. "I'll go to dinner, we'll talk, and that will be that. Hopefully by this time next week, I'm on the beach in Tel Aviv."

*

I checked my reflection one last time in the mirror before heading out. I had chosen a simple black sheath dress with three-quarter sleeves and a favourite pair of boots. I left my hair loose, and it curled perfectly. I was forced to admit I looked great. I didn't even bother with make-up—just a little lipstick to bring some colour.

Matt knew I was seeing Josh that night. We

spoke or texted almost daily. Josh was generally off-limits, but I had told him the week before when we were seeing each other, and I highly doubted he'd just forgotten. The previous night on the phone, he'd asked me if I thought it was possible to love two people at once.

"You're getting ahead of yourself," I said. "I love *you*."

"But do you think it's possible?"

"I'd imagine it is. My favourite TV show is based entirely on that premise."

"That's not helping," Matt said.

"Pick up a kilt. You'll be guaranteed to win."

He laughed.

"That's not funny," he said.

"You're the one who laughed."

"Nerves."

That night, as I prepared to meet Josh, I understood how Matt felt. I was going to meet the man I had thought I'd spend the rest of my life with. The man who told me he loved me but couldn't commit. We didn't fight, we didn't get petty—we just agreed we needed to end it, both of us still deeply in love. And then I met Matt.

I took one last look in the mirror, grabbed my purse and coat, and headed downstairs to meet my cab.

*

I walked into the downtown restaurant, one of the ones Josh and I used to frequent, and the one place I hadn't returned to since that last time I was there with him. It was our place, and I'm not sure it was wise to agree to meet him there. He was pulling out all the stops.

The maitre d' led me to the table and there he was, just as I'd remembered him. Josh stood up to greet me and we both stood there for a moment, not knowing whether to shake, hug, or kiss. I laughed to break the tension and leaned in to give him a peck on the cheek. We sat down.

He was wearing a brown sweater paired with light blue jeans. His hair was cut close, as always. It suited him—he had a beautifully-shaped head. Ridiculous, but true. He had a light growth on his beard, which was very unlike him. Josh always preferred a clean shave.

"So," Josh asked, cutting to the chase. "To what do I owe this honour?"

"You were very persistent, and I felt I owed it to you to hear what you had to say."

He looked at me, mildly surprised.

"And your boyfriend?"

"He's not here."

Josh nodded slowly.

The waiter came over and Josh gave our drink orders. He turned back to me.

"What's his name?"

"Matt. Matt Goldberg."

Josh laughed.

"You really like the Jewish boys, don't you."

I said nothing.

"Are you two serious?"

"Josh, I'm not here to talk about him. I'm here for you right now. What is so urgent? What brought you to my doorstep on my birthday?"

"I miss you, Allie."

"You're not dating?"

"I am," he admitted. "But it's not the same. I don't want them. I want you."

"I wanted you."

"Wanted."

"Josh. We talked about this. We talked it to death."

The waiter returned with our drinks and Josh gave me a quick glance. I gave a nod and he turned to the waiter and ordered dinner for both of us. He knew what I liked at that restaurant and was enjoying the opportunity to show me he remembered.

He turned back to me and put both hands on

the table.

"Allie, I grew up in a shitty household. You know that. My parents hated each other. Their marriage was miserable. And I got to witness that every day. You can't blame me for not wanting to repeat their mistakes."

"So marrying me would have been a mistake?"

"Well, that's the thing. I'm starting to think no."

I put down my glass and stared at him.

"You want to get married?" I said, astonished.

"I do."

I felt winded, like someone had punched me in the gut. I felt the colour drain from my face so I wasn't surprised when Josh reached over to me in alarm.

"Are you going to faint?" he asked.

"I just might," I said.

But those few words managed to ground me and I found my breath again. I steadied myself against the table and looked at him.

"Josh—"

"I know, it's a lot."

I bark-laughed so loud the couple at the next table looked over in disgust.

"And a little out of the blue," Josh continued.

"A little? So what happened, you dated a few

loser girls and realized it didn't get much better than me? Decided you didn't want to be alone the rest of your life? Start feeling the urge for kids? All of the above?"

"It's not like that, Allie. I never stopped loving you. And I don't think you stopped loving me."

"I don't know how I feel about you," I said, legitimately confused.

I put my hand up to rub my forehead and he reached across the table to take it. I let him. He held my hand between his for a few minutes, both of us silent. I focused on that hand, trying to decipher how it made me feel to have him touch me again. Still, the theme of the night was confusion.

"I don't know if I can eat, Josh."

"Allie, you promised me dinner. Let's just put this aside and enjoy a pleasant evening, okay?"

"I can try," I said.

As if on cue, the waiter arrived with our food and we spent the next few minutes eating in silence. Eventually, I broke the ice and asked him about work. He was in finance—high-pressure stuff that always left him on edge. He loved his work, but it stressed him out when the markets were down. We talked about that for a while until he turned the tables and asked me about my work.

"Is everything okay with your writing?" he asked.

"Yes, of course. Why do you ask?"

"Well, I haven't seen any of your reviews lately."

"Ah," I said. "I've actually been doing some ghostwriting."

"Ghostwriting? But Allie, you're so talented. You should write your own stuff."

I just smiled and kept eating. By the time we got through dessert and a bottle of wine, we were both feeling much more at ease with each other.

"Did you drive?" he asked after paying the bill.

"No, you?"

"No. Let's share an Uber."

"We could call a cab."

Josh rolled his eyes.

"Are we going to argue about this tonight?"

"No."

I had a thing against Uber, on many different fronts. But Josh had no patience for that. Any progress was good in his eyes. As long as we kept moving forward. It was one of the major differences between us.

We left the restaurant and the car was already waiting. Josh gave me a self-satisfied smirk. I had to laugh. He was cute. At this point, my confusion was full-force. We had talked about so much over dinner and it felt nice to be with him again. I realized he was on his best behaviour, but I liked his best behaviour.

When we got to my apartment, Josh asked the driver to wait and he walked me up to the door. I was relieved, having secretly been dreading him waiting for an invitation inside. I definitely wasn't ready for that. We walked up to the door I turned to thank him for dinner. Before I knew what was happening, he had his index finger under my chin and was pulling me in for a kiss.

When it landed, I automatically opened my mouth to let him in. He dropped his hands and pulled me closer, deepening his kiss. I reached up and took his face in my hands. The kiss was nice. I closed my eyes, and when I did, all I could see was Matt. My eyes flew open and I backed away.

"Josh—"

"It's okay. Too soon. I'll call you."

"Okay."

I turned and walked into the building, closing the door gently behind me. I wouldn't see him again. At least not by choice. I may have loved him once, but that had been nothing compared to the love I felt for Matt. It was startlingly clear. There was simply no comparison.

I walked up the two flights of stairs, into my apartment, dropped my coat on the floor, and continued on to the kitchen. Loki was with Trish for the night. Trish still hadn't moved out, anticipating my departure to Israel and a free place to crash for a few months. I had been completely on board with the plan, and that was a whole other source of guilt. I had thought I'd be gone weeks ago. She was going stir crazy with her parents.

I pulled out my box and rolled a joint. When I was done, I sat down at the kitchen table with an ashtray and opened my laptop. I lit the joint, took a few minutes to enjoy it, then started to write. When I was done, I read the piece over and sent it off to my editor, asking her to swap it out for whatever she'd planned to run that week. Then I got up and went to bed.

CHAPTER TWELVE

A few days later, I was lying in bed scrolling through my feed when my phone buzzed. The caller ID flashed Lynn and I answered right away.

"Yes?" I said.

"What are you doing for breakfast? Get up. Let's go eat."

"Lynn? What time is it?"

"It's ten o'clock. Get up. We'll meet at L'Oeufrier on Somerled. You can have that roll filled with scrambled eggs, chorizo and goat cheese you like so much."

I sat up in bed. She had me there.

"I'll be there in half an hour."

*

Lynn was waiting at our usual table when I got to the restaurant. We adored this place. The woman who ran it was so sweet and always remembered our favourite orders—right down to the smoothies and how I liked my potatoes. I sat down and Lynn wasted no time in getting to the point of the meeting.

"How did you do that? And why?" she asked.

"What?" I asked, legitimately confused. "What are you talking about?"

"I read your piece this morning. How did you make erotica sad? And why? Why would you do that?"

"Sad? It was a masturbation piece."

"Allie. It was a piece about you missing your boyfriend. I cried."

I looked at her like she was crazy.

"Lynn, even if that's true, you're the only one who would've picked that up."

"The *only* one?" she asked.

I ignored her and smiled at the waitress as she came over with our dishes. They must have started preparing the meals when they saw Lynn sit down.

"So how did it go with Josh?" Lynn asked, trying very hard to sound nonchalant.

She pushed her fork around in her potatoes while she waited for an answer.

"It was pleasant. But it's over. I'm not 100 percent sure he realizes that, but I do. I would very much like to get on the next flight to Tel Aviv."

Lynn burst into a smile.

"I knew it. I KNEW it. Oh, Allie. So when are you leaving?"

"I don't know. I tried Matt this morning but couldn't reach him. I took a few days to process everything before calling him. I really haven't spoken to him all week."

"That's unusual, isn't it?" Lynn asked.

"It is, but we both knew what was going down and maybe he was just nervous to call. I should've called him earlier."

"So? Just get on a plane. That's what you did last time."

"I could, but what if he's somewhere else at the moment? He might be traveling. I'll stay put until I hear back from him. My last surprise arrival didn't pan out so well, remember?"

The last time I showed up on Matt's doorstep unannounced, I was greeted by Maja, a tall, leggy Swedish blond. I freaked out and it took Matt and me 24 hours to smooth things out.

Lynn put a forkful of eggs in her mouth and shrugged.

"Things are different now. But wait if you want. I'll tell Dave to let Matt know you're looking for him."

I dug into my breakfast, smiling to myself at the thought of sunsets on the beach with my man.

*

By early afternoon the next day, I still hadn't heard from Matt. I was starting to get worried. It *was* Israel. Maybe something had happened to him. I shook my head, ridding myself of that horrible thought. But I couldn't drive the idea from my mind. I was ruminating over all the grisly possibilities when my phone rang. I jumped up and ran down the hall, finding it on the coffee table.

I picked it up, breathless, not even bothering to check the caller ID.

"Hello?"

"Allie."

It was Josh. *Shit*. I guess he hadn't figured it out.

"Hi, Josh."

"Listen, I was wondering if maybe you'd like to grab dinner again this week?"

I sat down on the couch.

"Josh, listen. It was great seeing you. And I had a nice evening. But I don't think anything is going to happen with us. It's too late. I've moved on."

"It's the other guy."

"It's me, and the other guy. I'm sorry, Josh. We had our time, and that time has passed. I'm going to hang up now."

"There's nothing I can say?" he asked.

"No. Nothing."

I put down my phone and looked at it for a moment. I smiled to myself, reflecting on the fact that Matt had been right. I *did* feel a great sense of closure.

I walked into the kitchen and turned on some music, loud. I was in the mood to celebrate. I opened the fridge and pulled out some eggs, deciding on a celebratory omelet. I assembled on the ingredients on the counter and paused, hearing a noise.

"Loki? That you?"

Trish had once again taken the dog, and I had been sure she said she'd be back around six. I checked the clock on the stove, which read 2:30 p.m. Curious, I walked out of the kitchen to see what was going on.

Matt stood in the hallway, a small overnight bag in hand, which he dropped to the floor the moment he saw me. I stood, paralyzed, unable to believe what I was seeing.

"Matt?" I asked, stupidly.

"Do you want me, Allie?"

"Of course I want you."

He crossed the hall in two strides and grabbed me around the waist, pulling me close and kissing me deeply, urgently. I wrapped my arms around his neck, pressing myself up against him, my body hungering for his. He pulled back slightly and pulled my shirt over my head while I frantically worked the button and zipper on his jeans. I bent to pull down while he tried to pull up and we got momentarily tangled. I laughed, breathless, and took a step backwards.

I undid my jeans and stepped out of them while he undid the buttons on his shirt, and removed my bra and panties while he slid his boxers down. Within thirty seconds, we were both naked and staring at each other. We were drawn to each other as if by a magnet, and before I knew what was happening, our hands were all over each other and he was whispering in my ear.

"God, I've missed you. I have ached for you. I never want to be without you again."

It was the best foreplay I'd ever had. I ran my hands up his back, over his neck, burying my fingers in his too-long curls.

"Up or down?" he asked.

"I don't care."

He pushed me up against the wall and held my wrists up by my head while he kissed me. It was the kind of kiss that only comes after being apart for over a month. It was full of love, longing, and most of all, lust. I returned it heartily. He let go of my wrist and reached down to lightly stroke me between the legs.

"Not necessary," I laughed, breaking the kiss.

He took the opportunity to bend down and take my nipple in his mouth, making quick swirls with his tongue that sent me swooning. He stood back up and reached down to guide himself in, and in a million years I couldn't describe the feeling when he slid home. I was complete.

He moved his hands under my ass and lifted, prompting me to wrap my legs around his waist while he thrust into me against the wall. I cried out and I felt him smile against my ear.

"Christ, I've missed those sounds," he whispered before taking my earlobe between his teeth.

I cried out again.

*

"What are you doing here?" I asked him a few minutes later. We were lying on the hallway floor, covered by his button-down shirt and my coat which we'd pulled down off the hook.

"You missed me," he said.

I got up on one elbow and looked down on him.

"What?"

"You missed me. I read your piece yesterday. It broke my heart. I got on the first flight back."

I burst out laughing.

"You and Lynn. She said she cried. It was a masturbation piece, for Christ's sake."

Matt just smiled at me, like he knew some deep secret he wasn't yet willing to share.

"You missed me."

We were silent for a few minutes, and I snuggled in closer to him, wrapping my arms around him and savouring the smell of him, despite his thirteen hours of travel.

"And the whole time I was gone, you only wrote about me," he added quietly.

"I kissed him," I blurted out, and immediately began to cry. All the guilt I'd been holding in for the week just came pouring out in those tears. Matt held me closer and stroked my hair.

"It's okay. It was my stupid idea to leave you here. I practically threw you at him."

"No, Matt," I protested. "You were right. I needed that closure. Now all three of us know where we stand."

He lifted my chin and gazed at me with so much love in his eyes I thought I'd burst. He kissed my forehead, my nose, my lips. I sighed, wrapping my arms tighter around him.

"How long are you here for?" I asked.

"We leave in three days."

"We?"

"I'm not going anywhere without you."

CHAPTER THIRTEEN

We flew from Montreal to Toronto before settling in for the long-haul flight to Tel Aviv. Matt used his points to upgrade me to business class so we could sit together. Being an experienced traveler, he came fully equipped to take care of both of us, right down to the gummies we popped before boarding the plane.

I had never been to the Middle East before and was eagerly anticipating the trip. I had booked a two-month ticket and we agreed we'd take it from there. I wasn't sure I was ready to spend the next four and half months so far from home, but neither of us was certain we'd want to be apart, either.

"Excited?" Matt asked as he pulled a magazine out of his bag.

"I am. What's the itinerary for the next few days?"

"Well, we land in Tel Aviv so I figured we'd spend the day and night there, then head back to Jerusalem for the weekend. The timing is great, because I have to be in Tzfat next week, and I think you'll love it there."

"The mystical city in the mountains? Sign me up!"

I reached into my bag and pulled out my headphones, intending to watch a movie until the gummy kicked in and I fell asleep.

"Allie?"

"Yeah?"

"You never wrote about, uh, your birthday."

I pulled out an earbud and looked him in the eye.

"I will *never* write about my birthday."

He smiled and kissed me on top of the head.

"Thank you."

"Hey," I said. "My goal is not to embarrass you. My goal is to write hot erotica. And to be honest, I think I paint you in a pretty good light."

"Oh, you do. I hear about it non-stop from Dave." Matt laughed.

"And *I* thought my birthday was pretty hot.

And if I recall correctly, you were not complaining. In fact, I heard you make noises I'd never heard before—"

"Okay," he interrupted. "Point taken."

I leaned over in my seat and brushed my lips up against his ear.

"I've missed your tight little ass."

Matt pulled away and turned beet red.

"Shut up," he said, picking up his magazine.

I popped my earbud back in and turned on the monitor, settling on a romantic comedy. I reclined into a semi-prone position and Matt reached over to lay a blanket over me. This was going to be amazing.

*

We landed by 11:00 a.m. and a car picked us up to take us to our hotel. Matt had booked a place right on the beach. As soon as we dumped our bags, Matt told me to change into a bathing suit.

"Can't we just have a little nap?" I asked.

"Absolutely not. We're going to the beach, then we'll have a nice dinner. I'm taking you to Forel, this amazing fish place. You'll love it."

"Mmm. That does sound good. Give me five minutes."

Twenty minutes later we were out the door

and our feet were in the sand. It was surreal, to have gone from the melting snow in Montreal to an unseasonably warm day in Tel Aviv for early April. The beach was populated but not packed. It was still off-season, and a workday. Matt and I spread out our towels but before I had the chance to lie down, he took me by the hand and led me towards the water.

I groaned but followed him into the ocean. The water wasn't too cold and it felt great after our long flight. We waded in together, chest high, and he took me around the waist and pulled me close.

"I want to travel with you like this forever," he said.

"Forever is a very long time."

"Allie. Stop it."

"He asked me to marry him."

Matt dropped his hands. He tilted his head and eyed me, trying to get a read.

"I can only assume you said no."

"I didn't say yes. But I never really got a chance to think about it, because the moment he kissed me, I knew there was nothing there."

"You mean, it didn't feel like this?"

Matt leaned in and kissed me. I put my hands on his hips and got on my tiptoes to fully return it, giving myself to him in that moment. He gathered me up in his arms and we stood there in the water making out for god knows how long. The sea air was like a drug and I could taste the salt on his skin. In the distance, I could vaguely hear the sounds of another couple laughing and splashing, but all of my attention was on Matt. When we finally pulled away from each other, I took a deep breath and laughed nervously.

"No, it didn't feel like that," I said.

We spent the rest of the afternoon at the beach, lazing in the sun and getting ice cream cones from Yotvata, a kibbutz-run business that had a storefront on the boardwalk. It was out of this world. That combined with the cheese I found on the hospitality plate in our room led me to believe that this country was going to have a lot to offer in the way of excellent dairy.

Later, Matt took me to dinner as promised. Also as promised, the food was spectacular. We shared a bottle of wine then walked through the streets of the city, all the way down to the ports at Jaffa. I could have moved there in a heartbeat. It was so modern, so alive, and right on the freaking beach. It was a total party city and I fell flat-out in love.

We got back to the room after nine and for the first time in memory, Matt and I fell asleep in the same bed without having sex. And that wasn't an exaggeration. I was on the pill and never got a period, so we were pretty much batting a hundred—save for the few nights before he left. But that night we were both so exhausted and jet-lagged we passed out before ten o'clock.

At some point in the night, I woke with a start. I was in a strange bed, and it took me a few seconds to get my bearings. As my eyes adjusted to the darkness, I looked around the room. It was quite nice—modern with little touches like chargers in all the sockets and a comfy chair by the window overlooking the ocean.

I turned to my left and saw Matt lying beside me, facing me, eyes wide open. I gave a little scream. He just laughed.

"What are you doing?" I asked.

"Waiting for you to wake up."

"How long have you been up?"

"About half an hour, I guess."

I sighed.

"Matt, once again, you can touch me when I'm sleeping. If I'm not in the mood, I'll let you know."

He shook his head.

"Matt, for Christ's sake. I am giving you permission."

"And what if you feel violated, waking up while I'm in the middle of having sex with you?"

"I can't think of anything hotter."

"I don't know, Allie."

I sighed again and then rolled my eyes for added effect. I pushed him onto his back and straddled him around the waist. He decisively put his hands on my hips and pulled me down, rolling over on top of me.

"Oh, no, you don't," he said. "I flew halfway across the world to collect you. I'm on top."

I howled with laughter until he covered my mouth with his, with considerably more force than I'd anticipated. My back arched instinctively and I wrapped my arms around his neck. There was hunger in his kiss and it stirred something deep within me. I moaned, raising my hips and grinding myself against him.

He broke the kiss and bent down to nip at my neck while pulling my T-shirt over my head. I then returned the favour and took a moment to run my hands down his back. He had a smattering of tight curly hair on his chest, but his back was completely smooth and just the feel of it sent a thrill through my body.

I worked his boxers down over his hips and he lifted himself off of me for a moment to complete the task. I took the opportunity to wiggle out of my panties, but he stopped me and pulled them down himself, pausing to kiss me briefly between the legs then blow softly. I let out another moan.

"I love when you do that," he murmured.

"Ditto," I sighed.

He climbed back on top of me, but rather than entering me right away, he began to move slowly, fully erect, against me. It was the most incredible sensation and I threw my head back, feeling his hard cock rub against my clit over and over. I raked his back with my nails as my hips rose to meet him and just as I was about to come, he pulled back suddenly and thrust himself inside.

I exploded around him immediately and cried out as he began to move in and out, building up a rhythm I couldn't match while in the throes of my orgasm. Before I had a chance to catch up to him, I felt him come and wrapped my legs around his waist, drawing him in closer, letting him fill me completely. He collapsed against my chest, breathing heavily into my neck.

After a moment, I began to make fake suffocating noises and he chuckled and rolled over onto his back.

"Have I ever told you you're the greatest fuck I've ever had?" he asked.

"Say it again," I laughed.

"You are the greatest fuck I have ever had."

CHAPTER FOURTEEN

The next day, we packed up and left for Jerusalem. It was a quick drive—the country is tiny—and we got back to Matt's apartment in time to grab a quick lunch. We went to a famous hummus place, a concept I'd never even contemplated before. After a few dishes, however, I made a mental note to call Sarah and pitch her a piece on Middle Eastern fare. Still tired after our travels, we spent the rest of the day at home.

Matt's apartment was simple and sparse, but contained everything he needed to live comfortably. It was a one-bedroom with a decent-sized living room and a small but functional kitchen. Once again his living room contained a killer couch, and as soon as I saw it I was drawn to it as if by tractor beam. Matt smiled at me as I sank into the plush upholstery and propped my feet up on the ottoman.

"Two thumbs up!" I said.

He came over to join me and we spent the afternoon watching old movies. I was a Hepburn/Tracy sucker, and he was all about Bogart and Bacall. I was fine with that, as it meant the majority of the films we ended up watching would be mine. They had the larger catalog.

Matt made me an easy dinner of pasta with olive oil and garlic. We split a bottle of white wine and it was perfect. After we ate, he pulled Scrabble off the shelf, the only board game in the entire apartment. We played drunk Scrabble for a couple of hours until neither of us could keep our eyes open. I don't even remember getting up from the table, but we must have because the next thing I knew I was waking up in bed at 10 o'clock in the morning. I shot straight up.

"Good morning, Sunshine," Matt said, walking into the room with a cup of hot tea for me.

"Is that mint I smell?"

"Israeli specialty."

He placed the cup on the bedside table and sat down. He picked up my hand and held it between his own.

"How long have you been up?" I asked.

"Not long, maybe an hour. I guess we both slept through the night."

"Did we fuck?"

Matt laughed.

"No. We didn't." He eyed me. "You owe me one."

He moved up the bed toward me but I put up my hand to stop him. I pushed the covers down and slid my legs around him, landing my feet on the floor.

"I have to pee," I said.

I picked up the cup of tea and took it with me into the bathroom. I closed the door, looked in the mirror, and rubbed my eyes. I needed that sleep, but I still looked exhausted. I rummaged through my cosmetics bag and pulled out my birth control pills. I looked at the packet and popped out the Friday pill, washing it down with a swig of tepid tea. I grimaced.

When I was done in the bathroom I rejoined Matt in the bedroom, only to find him pulling on his jeans and a T-shirt.

"Where we going?" I asked.

"Going? We're not going anywhere. It's Shabbat. Nothing happens in Jerusalem today.

Unless you want to go pray."

"Shabbat? I thought that was on Saturday."

"It is on Saturday. Today is Saturday."

"Today is Friday."

Matt laughed.

"No. The flight messed you up. I'm just going to go into the kitchen and whip up some breakfast."

Matt walked out of the room and I sat down on the bed, suddenly unable to breathe. *It's okay*, I told myself. *I only screwed up the past three days.* I calmly got up, but immediately sat back down as I broke into a sweat and felt sick. *You will not throw up.* I got up slowly and walked into the bathroom, sprinting the last few steps and barely making it to the toilet.

Holy shit. I stood up and walked over the sink where I brushed my teeth for a good three minutes. I then pulled out my pack of pills, popped Saturday's out of the foil, and dry-swallowed it. Then I walked back into the bedroom and called Lynn.

"Allie? What the fuck? Is everything okay? It's 3 a.m."

"No. Everything is not okay. I fucked up my pills. And when I realized I fucked up my pills, I threw up. So then I took another pill to compensate. I'm a fucking mess. What do I do?"

"Calm down," Lynn said, as the sleep cleared from her voice. "How many days did you miss?"

"Just one. Three days ago."

"Well," she said. "Maybe just blow him for the next few days or so, until you're back on track."

I was silent for a moment.

"That's actually excellent advice."

"Happy to help. Good night."

I put my phone down and joined Matt in the kitchen.

*

On Sunday evening, Matt took me to a great steakhouse just a little past the Mahane Yehuda market. As soon as we sat down, Matt started ordering in Hebrew, a skill I hadn't even known he possessed. It was hot. Moments later, waiters appeared at our table with a dozen small plates filled with various salads. That was soon followed by morsels of the most tender steak I'd ever had. I was in heaven.

"Rumour has it that the restaurant across the street is owned by this guy's brother. Big family feud or something." Matt said.

"Hmph," I said, my mouth way too full to engage in conversation.

When we were done, the waiters reappeared and piled all the dishes on their arms until they resembled blooming flowers. It was the most spectacular thing I'd ever seen in a restaurant, especially one so plain in appearance.

We walked back to the apartment hand in hand, passing by the market to pick up some earth-shattering chocolate rugulach from a bakery called Marzipan. Matt's AirBnB was in the area of Abu Tor, just past the old train station. It was a lovely walk, mostly downhill until we got to the last stretch. That was a killer. At least I was working off all the food I was eating.

As we walked through the front door, Matt turned to me.

"We should pack up tonight. Enough for the week. I have a feeling you'll want to stay through the weekend in Tzfat. And I got us a killer room at the Rimonim Hotel."

"Sounds great."

I walked through to the bedroom and pulled a small bag out of the closet. I packed up some clothes, my Kindle, and my laptop, then quickly undressed and got into bed. Matt came in a little while later and eyed me.

"You're in bed early," he said.

"Come join me."

He walked towards me and started stripping

off his clothes.

"You don't have to ask me twice," he said.

When he got to the bed, I swung my legs over the side and stopped him from climbing in. He looked at me, quizzically. I sat on the edge of the bed, placing one leg on either side of him as he faced me. He put his hands on top of my head and I took him in my mouth. He sighed as he buried his fingers in my hair. I held him by the hips as I worked my tongue down his shaft and back up to the tip, making increasingly larger circles with my tongue until finally taking him back into my mouth.

"Allie…"

I smiled around him and continued. It took less than five minutes for him to come in my mouth, calling my name as he did. I loved when he did that. It meant I'd done well.

CHAPTER FIFTEEN

Matt had been right. I fell for Tzfat the moment we started the uphill drive through the mountains in the rental car. It was breathtaking. And then we pulled up into this tiny mountaintop village made up of alleyways, cobblestone streets, and artist colonies. It was unreal.

And the hotel? Spectacular. We had a beautiful suite with stone walls, like it had been carved out of a cave. It was the most romantic place we'd ever been, though the houseboat in Amsterdam was a close second.

We spent the day walking through the city, visiting the ancient synagogues, and going up and down the steps that wound their way through the mountain. We visited art galleries and I bought a few small things I knew would always remind me of our time here, including a gorgeous watercolour of an old lamp post in an alley. We grabbed a light dinner and headed back for the night.

When we got back to the hotel, I immediately peeled off my clothes and ran the water in the tub.

"Come take a bath with me," I said.

Matt appeared in the doorway and started unbuttoning his shirt when his phone rang. He picked it up, listened for a few minutes, and frowned.

"Yeah, okay," he said. "I'll be there in a few minutes."

He hung up and looked at me apologetically as he buttoned up his shirt.

"I'm sorry. I'll be back as soon as I can. Try to wait up for me."

I smiled and climbed into the tub, soaping up my boobs for him before he turned to leave.

"Allie…"

"Hurry home."

After a luxurious soak, I wrapped myself in the ultra-lux bathrobe, grabbed the weed tin, and climbed into bed. I flipped on the TV and was delighted to discover my favourite show in Hebrew. The Scottish accent was missing, but as long as those muscles were still there, I was all good. I rolled a joint and smoked it leisurely, waiting for Matt to get back.

The bath, combined with the day's activity and the weed, knocked me out. I was fast asleep by the end of the episode. I went from my hotel bed in Tzfat to walking through the doors of the cabin on the Ridge, wearing only my shift. As I entered the one-room house, I saw my red-headed hero sitting on the bed, waiting for me. I pulled at the string above my breasts and slipped my shoulders out of the shift, letting it fall and gather at my feet.

I walked over to him and he reached up to take my hands in his. He pulled me down towards him and I sighed in my sleep, rolling over and unconsciously running my hands over my breasts. He leaned over and kissed me, first on my forehead, then on my nose, and finally on my lips. It was so gentle, so soft, I couldn't help but kiss him back. I wrapped my arms around him and felt him climb on top of me, those strong Highlander arms closing around me.

I moaned and parted my legs, raising my hips in invitation. My head swam as he slid in, moving slowly, almost hesitatingly, as he worked up a rhythm. I cried out softly, reaching up to stroke his curls.

"Open your eyes," he whispered in my ear.

"They are open," I said.

He chuckled softly.

"Open your eyes."

I realized he was right, and my eyes were closed. I opened them tentatively and found Matt on top of me, staring at me with amusement in his eyes. I picked up my head and kissed the smile off his face, increasing the speed of my hips as I realized my dream had been no dream. Just the lead actor was different. I moved my hands to his ass and Matt shifted positions slightly until he heard me moan, then he drove it home. We came together, and I wrapped myself around him, holding him close until the last waves of the orgasm left my body.

"Okay," he said, wonder in his voice. "Maybe that was a little hot."

"Told you," I laughed. "I wonder if I was dreaming first, or if you came in first."

"Oh, you were definitely dreaming. The way you were running your hands over your tits, I was hard by the time I hit the bed."

I laughed again, then suddenly sat up. *Oh my god*. We'd had sex. That was not the plan. I should've told him. But I couldn't tell him then. I had spent hours arguing that he could accost me in my sleep; I couldn't lay this on him now. No. I'd keep my fingers crossed that everything would be okay. Just a tiny fuck up. One missed pill. How bad could it be?

"You okay?" he asked.

"Yeah, fine. I just have to pee."

I jumped out of bed and walked to the bathroom. I closed the door and sat down on the toilet, waiting for whatever he'd deposited to exit. I couldn't believe I'd actually wrapped myself around him. *Oy*, as he'd say. Whatever the situation, we wouldn't know for a month, so there was no point in worrying about it now. I decided I'd talk to him if there was something to talk about.

*

After we returned to Jerusalem, Matt got serious about work and I buckled down to do some writing. I had plenty of material to work with and my editor had been thrilled with me lately. Apparently, they'd upped their ad revenues as a result of the traffic I was bringing in. I still hadn't told my parents. I had decided it would be better to let them think Matt was funding my travel than confess the truth.

I wrote mainly in the mornings and spent my afternoons touring the city. There was so much to explore. The history was amazing, and it was surreal knowing that I was walking in the same paths as biblical figures. I did an underground tour of the Western Wall and went up to the Temple Mount to see the Al-Aksa Mosque. I went spelunking through caves. I scoured the market stalls in the Old City while eating as much falafel and shawarma as humanly possible. The food in that country was simply divine.

The weeks flew by. Matt and I spent every possible moment together and never seemed to grow tired of each other's company or each other's bodies. I knew from experience that the sex would eventually slow down, but it had been a solid six months now and it was showing no signs of abating. We had brought a few toys along and spent a few nights exploring new kinds of light kink. He really enjoyed tying me up and was experimenting with different positions. I had zero complaints.

One night, about ten days before I was to leave, I was on the bed, completely naked and on my knees. He had my wrists cuffed to my ankles behind me and was in the middle of trailing a light flogger down my chest. He paused and gave me a quick lash. I yelped. He stopped.

"You okay?"

"Yeah. Sorry. I don't know what that was all

about."

He looked at me, hesitating.

"It's fine," I insisted.

Internally, I was rolling my eyes. A little light bondage still presented some conflict for Mr. Consent, despite (or maybe because of) how much it turned him on.

He flicked the flogger again, this time hitting my other breast. And this time I cried out louder.

"Do we have a safe word?" I asked.

He dropped the flogger and unclipped the restraints within three seconds flat.

"What's the matter?" he asked.

"Not sure. My boobs hurt, that's all. Must be close to that time."

He raised his eyebrows and leaned forward to kiss me.

"Can we still fuck?"

"Of course we can," I said.

I pushed him back on the bed and climbed on top.

"Just don't touch my tits," I said, sliding onto him.

He reached forward and slipped a hand between my legs.

"That's okay," he said. "I can find other things to play with."

*

A while later, we were snuggling under the covers and I was just starting to drift off to sleep.

"Have you thought about staying?" Matt asked.

I opened my eyes and gave myself a moment to return to planet earth.

"What do you think I should do?" I asked.

He snorted.

"That's a stupid question. I want you to stay."

"You're not tired of me yet?"

"Allie, I could never be tired of you. I love you. I want to spend all my time with you. Like you said, I want to do everything with you."

"What are you saying? You see us growing old together, raising babies and rearing dogs?"

Matt laughed.

"That sounds delightful," he said, kissing me on the head.

"I don't know, Matt. I mean, that all sounds delightful to me, too, but right now, I'm thinking maybe I should get back home. Two months, plus the four months in Amsterdam. I feel bad about Sarah and Loki. And I do miss Lynn. Let me think about it."

He gave me a quick squeeze and I snuggled in closer, closing my eyes against his chest.

I woke the next morning on my stomach, again with my boobs in pain. My eyes flew open. Tender breasts? *Oh, shit.* I got up, careful not to disturb Matt. There were so few mornings he got to sleep in that I didn't want to wake him. I slipped on a T-shirt and a pair of sweats and went to the bathroom to clean up.

With Matt still sleeping, I slipped out the front door and walked to the bottom of the hill, where a corner store would hopefully be stocking pregnancy tests. By the time I got back, I had broken a serious sweat and was determined to head straight for the shower. I passed Matt in the kitchen, who was busy making breakfast.

"I picked up juice!" I said, handing him my alibi.

I continued to the bathroom and closed the door. I frantically pulled the pregnancy test out of the bag and pulled down my pants. I hadn't peed since the night before, opting to hold it this morning for the most accurate results. I sat down, slid the stick between my legs and let loose.

I sat there afterward until the buzzer on my phone timer went off. With shaking hands, I reached forward and picked up the test off the counter. I closed my eyes, took a deep breath, and opened them. I took a look.

Negative.

I sighed in relief and then burst into tears. *Tears?* What the fuck? It took me a moment, but I eventually realized I was actually disappointed. A part of me had *wanted* to have Matt's baby. The thought was insane, yet simultaneously true. He was perfect for me, and we were perfect together. Why wouldn't we make a perfect family? Maybe my joke from the night before hadn't been so funny.

I carefully wrapped the stick up in toilet paper and buried it in the wastebasket. I washed my hands and my face, then went to join Matt in the kitchen.

He was at the stove, stirring scrambled eggs in the pan, and looked up as I entered, a smile lighting up his face.

"Everything okay?" he asked.

"Everything is perfect," I said.

I walked over to him and wrapped my arms around his waist, resting my chin on his shoulder and watching him cook.

"In fact," I said. "I've decided to stay with you."

"To stay with me? That's amazing. For how long?"

He put down the wooden spoon and turned to gather me up in his arms and kiss me. I wrapped my arms around his neck and whispered in his ear.

"Forever."

Other books by Sydney Campbell:

Allie Styles Romance Series:
Temptation (Book 1)
Deception (Book 2)
Reckonings (Book 3)
Beginnings (Book 4)

Courtyard Tales of Contemporary Romance
Reawakening
Redemption
Reckless

www.ingramcontent.com/pod-product-compliance
Lightning Source LLC
Chambersburg PA
CBHW030750110726
47900CB00008B/2530